AVENGING ANGEL

by

Kevin O'Hagan

Grosvenor House
Publishing Limited

This book is published by
Grosvenor House Publishing Ltd
Link House
140 The Broadway, Tolworth, Surrey, KT6 7HT.
www.grosvenorhousepublishing.co.uk

This book is a work of fiction. Any resemblance to
people or events, past or present, is purely coincidental.

A CIP record for this book
is available from the British Library

ISBN 978-1-80381-978-5

Other Books by the Author

Battlescars
No Hiding Place
Last Stand
Killing Time
A Change of Heart
Blood Tracks
The Key to Murder
Murder in Store
Buried Secrets

For my wonderful family. Wishing you
continued health and happiness.

In memory of family and friends
who have passed.

Acknowledgements

As always, my huge thanks to the 'Usual Suspects', who helped me on my journey from getting this story from an idea to print.

My daughter Lauren for the proofreading, grammar and spellcheck.

My son Tom for yet another excellent cover design.

My publishers for all their help and guidance, especially Melanie Bartle.

My wife Tina for her continued support of my writing and the tea and coffee.

Author's Note

Some places and locations in this novel exist in real life; others are purely fictional, as may be their geographical placings. Landscapes, names and layouts take on another imaginary status in this book.

All the characters are purely fictional, as are their stories.

Thank you for indulging me to help in creating this story.

A Word from the Author

Well, here is my tenth novel. Who would have thought it? Not me certainly, yet here it is.

When I wrote my first novel *Battlescars*, I was over the moon with the accomplishment. After all, it's said that we all have a book inside of us.

To be able to carry on from there is a dream come true.

The ideas, the plots and the characters keep coming and as long as they do and you, the reader, keep supporting my stories, then I will try to keep going.

Writing has now become such a big part of my life that I can't envisage a day not writing in some shape or form.

To see an idea form in my mind, then materialise on a page and make that exciting journey into a story is a magical process and one I never grow tired of.

So, sit back, put your feet up and enjoy *Avenging Angel*.

It gives a shoutout to fictional comic book characters such as Batman and The Punisher. It also explores the age-old battle of good versus evil and the fine line that sometimes separates them.

The story has my usual trademark twists and turns and the same gritty dialogue as we once again delve into the darker side of humanity.

Kevin, April 2024

*"For we know Him who said,
'Vengeance is Mine, I will repay,' says the Lord.
And again, 'The Lord will judge his people'."*

Hebrews 10:30 (NKJV)

Michael the Archangel's mission:

*"Defend us in battle. Be our protector against
wickedness and the snares of the devil."*

Prologue

Helmand Province, Afghanistan, 2015

The SAS team closed in on the stone compound where members of the Taliban were meant to be hiding. The team was on a secret mission, a mission of their own undertaking built on personal intel given to them.

This would be a strike and run mission. In and out as quickly as possible.

The compounds they were approaching were the homes of Afghan families who normally had many young children under fifteen years of age living in them.

Recent US air strikes to many of these compounds, presumedly harbouring Taliban troops, had resulted in the untimely deaths of many youngsters.

This had sounded an outcry from the Afghan authorities about the legality of these strikes.

Number 10 and the Cabinet Office at home in the UK were also beginning to become perturbed about the behaviour of a small percentage of the SAS who seemed to be taking their own action against the Afghans.

Disquiet was circulating about up to 80 deaths from the SAS deployment in Helmand Province between 2010 and 2013, many of which involved the shooting dead of Afghan civilians on SAS night raids.

Concerns about conduct circulated within the SAS, with an inquiry citing emails describing one deadly incident as 'the latest massacre'.

That led eventually to the formation of Operation Northmoor in 2014, a military police inquiry into allegations of unlawful killings by the SAS in Afghanistan. By 2015, it was beginning to identify a small number of members of the elite unit for possible arrest, and the progress of the inquiry was shared with Downing Street.

Following the 9/11 terrorist attacks in America, Britain deployed to Afghanistan with the US and other allies to destroy al-Qaeda, and the Taliban who had backed them.

UK forces were deployed to Afghanistan in support of the UN-authorised, NATO-led International Security Assistance Force mission and as part of the US-led Operation Enduring Freedom. Between 2003 and the end of 2014, UK operations in Afghanistan were conducted under the name Operation Herrick.

Despite only being there to 'train, advise or assist' Afghan forces, members of the SAS and SBS had taken it upon themselves to be involved in lethal rogue night raids.

The Helmand area was one that the US and UK troops wanted to capture and control most as it supplied the country's biggest opium stores.

It was vital to winning this conflict and chasing off the Taliban.

The military forces were prepared to do what was needed, even if it didn't quite fit protocol.

Tonight, Team Wolf was on such a mission.

The team consisted of eight men, led by Captain Mick Lange.

The team's intelligence information had been sketchy to say the least, but the rogue team were ready to carry out this covert mission, nonetheless.

* * *

Captain Mick Lange brought his team to a halt at a distance from the compound and viewed it through night vision goggles.

They team had made this final part of their journey on foot, leaving their two vehicles some distance away out of sight.

It was 2:00am and all seemed quiet.

The plan was to catch the Taliban cold and take them out before they knew what had hit them.

The intelligence told them that at least 20 members were using this compound as a hideout.

Lange now looked at his assembled men.

They were a tight bunch and they had all worked successfully together on many occasions. They were a band of brothers. Tough soldiers, but also good mates.

"Right, we stick to this plan to the letter. We go in through the front door together, so we all know where we are and this stops us coming in at different directions and confusing things. There are four dwelling within the walls. We don't know for sure which ones the Taliban occupy. We sweep each building and all its rooms and take out the enemy. There's a high possibility of women and children being present as the Taliban are using them for cover. Remember, take out the bad guys only. Are we ready?"

The collective nodded.

"Right. Let's do it!" said Lange.

The team moved out swiftly, working under the cover of darkness and moving stealthily towards the compound.

Once in position, Lange gave the order.

The doors were blown in and the team entered.

They moved across the courtyard and split off into the buildings. Quickly and efficiently, they searched every room and found the compound completely empty. There was no trace of human life.

This was puzzling.

Had their information been incorrect? Or had the enemy known somehow that they were coming and evacuated the building long before?

The team searched again, but found nothing.

After their initial confusion, they were disappointed. They had been ready for the kill.

That first burst of adrenaline that they experienced entering the building in anticipation had now subsided.

Lange pulled the men together.

"Alright, guys. It looks like we've lucked out and received bad intelligence. Time to call it a night and head back."

The men nodded and headed for the front door.

The team were gutted that they hadn't seen action tonight.

They saw themselves as righters of wrong. Saviours. Men who fought for justice and good. They were men that would do whatever it took to succeed and finish their mission.

They lived and breathed the job.

There was much evil and wickedness in this world and if it wasn't for men like these, the evils would overpower and consume all that was good.

There were times when talking and negotiations did not cut it. When politics, rules and regulations were no longer the answer. This was where these men and their like came in. To cut out a cancer, you were going to shed some blood.

Captain Mick Lange was on his second tour of Afghanistan. He had seen plenty of bloodshed on both sides. He was also a veteran of the Iraq War.

War could be a nasty and unpleasant business for sure, but Lange and his team were good at it. The best.

Lange loved the Armed Forces. There was nothing better for him.

From the time he was a youngster of twelve gazing in the window of the army recruitment office, he knew that, when he was old enough, he would become a soldier.

* * *

As the team gathered in the courtyard and prepared to leave, a noise from behind stopped them in their tracks and made them spin around.

Lange saw a trapdoor in the ground spring open and rocket propelled grenades came flying out.

Then, several men's faces appeared with automatic M249 machine guns drawn.

The clever bastards had been hiding in an underground tunnel.

They had known that the SAS were coming and had outfoxed them due to the incorrect intel given to Team Wolf. Now they were going to pay the price.

* * *

It all seemed to happen in slow motion.

Lange yelled a warning, but it was too late. The grenades went off with concussive explosions.

Lange was lifted and thrown back by the force. He smashed the back of his head on the stone wall of the compound, which stunned him. He lay dazed and watched as his team was ripped apart.

Limbs were torn away and bodies exploded in a mix of crimson and viscera.

The few who survived the explosions tried to deploy their weapons, but were cut down by automatic gun fire.

Lange saw his team, his comrades and his friends destroyed in the most horrific way.

Tough men, good soldiers, just wasted in the blink of an eye.

He glimpsed to his left and saw the youngest member of his team, Joe Eccles, crawling towards him. His face displayed extreme pain and his mouth moved in a silent plea.

Lange had taken it on himself to look out for this man as he knew his family well from back in the day. He had gone to school with Joe's mother and brother and had remained good friends, even though they went different ways in their careers.

When Joe joined Lange's team and he found out who he was, he promised to take care of him. Joe was a competent soldier, but Lange still found that he was always watching the younger man's back.

Lange could now see that both Joe's legs were missing. He reached out his hand towards his friend. Their fingers met momentarily and then a bullet blew half of Joe's face away.

Lange cried out in anguish as the younger man's blood sprayed his own face.

As battle hardened as he was, Lange momentarily froze in horror.

Joe was gone.

He then felt the heat and weight of bullets pierce his own body.

With adrenaline coursing through his veins and the will to survive, he scrambled to his feet and staggered out of the exit.

There was nothing he could do now for his team. It was all down to self-preservation.

Although in extreme pain, his body was jacked with a cocktail of hormones all designed to help him live.

The explosions had damaged Lange's eardrums. He was bleeding from both. He felt that he had been hit twice with bullets somewhere on his torso, but he was still alive. He also had pain in his left leg where some shrapnel had lodged into his calf.

Lange staggered off into the enveloping darkness of the night, hoping that he would find cover to help get him back to safety.

His mind was in turmoil after the brutal and unexpected attack. He was shocked to the core that all his good mates were gone.

Especially Joe.

What would he tell his mother if he got out of here alive?

He and the others had died on his watch. He had been their Captain, which made him responsible.

He then asked himself the question why had he survived?

As he stumbled on in the dark, he heard himself say, "Please God help me. Don't let me die here alone. Why have I survived?"

He hadn't prayed to God since he was a kid, but now, here in the dark all alone, it felt like the right thing to do.

His life was slowly ebbing away.

He needed to keep moving...

Chapter 1

17 December 2023, 1:00am, Bristol city centre

"Fuck you, Trent. I'm going home. You're an asshole! Do you know that?" screamed Dawn Little.

She barged her way out of the Pacifica nightclub.

She was drunk and angry. She needed to get away from the club and put some distance between herself and Trent.

She brushed back her blonde hair from her eyes and buttoned her coat.

It was cold outside and fine flakes of snow were falling. Christmas was just around the corner.

All she wanted now was to get home to her flat and shut the world out.

Trent Lewis appeared at the club entrance. His handsome, black features showed concern.

"Dawn. Dawn. I'm sorry. Come back. Please. I'm sorry. It was nothing. Okay?"

He was also drunk. He stood swaying unsteadily on his feet.

Drunken revellers watched the scene unfold. Just another Saturday in Bristol city centre.

Season of good will or not, some people weren't ready to embrace it.

Dawn turned around at the sound of Trent's voice.

"I told you to fuck off. Now leave me alone. Go back and carry on chatting up those two little whores. Enjoy yourself. I'm out of here!"

Trent pleaded.

"Come on, Dawn. I wasn't doing anything. You're overreacting! It was just a kiss under the mistletoe. A bit of harmless fun. Nothing more."

"Get lost!" She spat as she turned and nearly lost her balance on her stiletto heels.

"Well, fuck you as well then, you bitch. Go and see if I care. I'll be selling your Christmas present on eBay tomorrow."

Trent stormed back into the club and disappeared into the heaving mass of people. He needed another drink.

Dawn walked away. She searched in her bag to see if she had any money left for a taxi, but she knew already that she had spent her last £10 on those last two gin and tonics. Her bank card was no good as the account was in the red.

"Shit," she muttered under her breath, "I'll just have to walk."

As she teetered up the road, she thought of Trent. The bastard.

They had been seeing each other on and off for two years now. To say that their relationship was volatile was an understatement.

She couldn't remember the number of times they had fallen out, broken up and then got back together again.

There were a dozen reasons that this happened: his womanising, his drinking, his online gambling habit. She just couldn't trust him.

But despite everything, they always somehow got back together.

Dawn Little was 27 years old and she was at the stage of her life where she wanted a bit more stability. Maybe to even settle down. Possibly marriage.

But Trent, although himself 28 years of age, was still like a kid. He just wanted to go out partying and clubbing. There was no hint of commitment.

Whenever she mentioned the subject, he found an excuse to avoid it.

She had grown tired of the pub and club life. Alcohol and cocaine were taking its toll, not only on her body, but also on her finances. Going out at the weekend and getting hammered had become the norm. She didn't particularly enjoy it anymore, but went along with it to please Trent.

Inevitably, they would both get smashed and either have a night to remember or both argue and fight. There was never any middle ground.

Well, fuck him. Tonight was the last straw. That was it. He won't come crawling back this time.

She had gone to the toilet in the club and when she came back, she had caught the bastard snogging with a couple of young tarts. No shame or remorse. Just doing it like she didn't exist.

No way would she forgive him for that. Never.

* * *

Dawn now walked on past groups of young people drinking in the streets or coming and going from takeaways and burger vans.

The main high street looked like a bombsite.

The festive season was coming. Spirits were high. People were singing, shouting and dancing around the pavements. Others were throwing up the contents of their stomachs spectacularly. Some were sat down on the cold ground, too wrecked to move. Others had completely collapsed. Comatose. Totally out of it.

Their Christmas had started a week early and was well and truly underway or down the toilet, depending how you looked at it.

Takeaway rubbish littered the place. It was hell on earth. Yet she was so often part of it. Now it all seemed disgusting.

A group of young lads staggered past her. One shouted.

"Alright love. Give us a blowjob?"

She told them where to go and carried on walking. She could hear their sniggers as they went on their way.

Dawn now passed by the entrance of the *Jungle Club*, a busy and well-known venue in the centre. She hadn't been in there for some time as it had gained a reputation for trouble in recent years.

Three doormen employed to stamp out the trouble stood at the entrance. Two black and one white.

The club was shutting and they were gradually guiding people out and on their way home.

The three were all veterans of the door and highly capable. The men were also well-known faces in the nightclub world and their formidable reputations succeeded them.

Most people sensibly gave them a wide berth. But once in a while, with the injection of booze and drugs, some fool would risk their ass looking to make a name for themselves.

Suddenly, three men burst out through the door shouting obscenities as they left.

The white doorman spoke.

"Right, on your way, lads. That's your lot. Get moving!"

The biggest of the three men, a blonde-haired guy, sneered back at him.

"Fuck you. What are you gonna do, asshole?"

The doorman sighed. It was a world-weary sigh from somebody who had seen and heard all this before. He glanced at his two colleagues. They were both huge men like himself. He looked back at the blonde guy.

"Look, we don't want a scene here, so go on home."

"Bollocks," shouted the guy.

Too much vodka had inflated his ego. Sober, he wouldn't have thought of crossing this monster of a man's path. But at this moment, his monkey brain had unfortunately hijacked his logical one.

The man had a Brummie accent. Obviously, he wasn't from around the area; otherwise, he would have known better than to pick a fight here.

He stormed towards the doorman, fist clenched. It was the move of an amateur.

His advance was stopped by a picture-perfect right cross that connected on his chin with sickening force. The fist that landed the punch had a brass knuckleduster on it.

The blonde guy hit the pavement like a dead thing, his jaw hanging at an unnatural angle. He would be eating his Christmas dinner through a straw. His prone body twitched a little before becoming still.

"Now pick him up and fuck off," said the doorman to the others.

They duly obliged, silenced by the brutality of the knockout. Their drunken brains found it hard to register what had just happened to their mate.

Tony Ellis looked at the two black guys, Errol White and Chris Comer. They all broke into laughter.

"You're a bad man, Tony. You aren't going to heaven, bro," grinned Errol.

Tony grinned.

"Don't you know, I sold my soul to the devil a long time ago…"

* * *

Dawn had watched the scene as if it had all happened in slow motion.

As she staggered past them, the alcohol numbed her senses and feelings to the sudden violence.

Tony immediately spotted her. She was a stunner, but looked a little worse for wear.

"Are you okay? You don't look so good," he said.

Dawn regarded him through blurry eyes.

"Yeah, I'm fine."

"Look, you don't want to be walking home alone at this hour. Get yourself in a taxi. I can order you one if you like."

"No, thanks. I want to walk. I need to sober up," she mumbled and staggered away.

Chris and Errol regarded Tony.

"Hey, I guess there's no helping some people."

Tony watched the disappearing figure of the girl.

She was a little peach, no doubt about that, but also a stupid girl wandering around alone at this hour. She was vulnerable and easy prey. He had seen it so many times.

Alcohol and other substances taking away any sense of caution and causing individuals to take unnecessary risks.

* * *

Across from the club, stood in the shadows, a man watched the scenario unfold with interest.

He dropped the remains of his cigarette to the pavement and crushed it under his boot. Then, he slowly walked across the road to follow the girl at a discreet distance.

The man was dressed head to toe in black. He was big. 6'2 and around a 102 kg.

He moved lightly and easily on his feet, although he walked with a slight limp. He blended into the shadows.

He passed the nightclub door. Casually, he eyed the three giant doormen.

Dangerous men, he mused. Men used to violence and men used to being top dogs. He had been around men like that in his past life.

These were men confident in their abilities. They were used to getting what they wanted.

In this world, you had the wolves and the sheep.

These men were definitely wolves.

The man in black thought of himself as the sheepdog.

* * *

As Dawn reached a quieter spot up the road, she sat down on a low wall. She suddenly felt sick. As her anger subsided, she started to cry.

That bastard Trent really did hurt her. What a waste of an evening. She had to get home to bed. She had had enough.

She would now plan to spend Christmas at her parents.

Come new year, she would make a fresh start for herself and get away from Bristol and her toxic lifestyle and relationship for good.

She knew deep down that her relationship with Trent wasn't destined to last and she had kidded herself for so long. Now she could see the wood for the trees.

Dawn now felt a little better about things.

Suddenly, she was aware of somebody standing beside her. She looked up with a start.

Then, she recognised the face.

"It's you. What do you want?"

"Well, I couldn't let you walk away on your own. It played on my mind, so I came looking for you."

She looked up into the face of the white doorman, Tony Ellis.

"Didn't your mates mind you leaving your post?"

"No," smiled Tony, "They can handle things without me. Plus, we've nearly finished our shift."

He extended his hand.

"Can I walk you somewhere?"

Dawn took the offered hand and rose to her feet.

"Thank you," she whispered, "This way."

They began to walk.

"So, what are you? Some sort of knight in shining armour? Helping ladies in distress."

Tony laughed.

"Yeah. Something like that."

"You do this for every girl that walks past looking a little vulnerable or lost, do you?"

"No, but there was something about you that made me want to come and help. Don't you feel vulnerable after the murder of that young girl here in Bristol a few months back?"

Dawn suddenly thought about this. She realised that, in her drunken rage at Trent, she had forgotten all about the terrible incident that had happened to a young girl in this area after a night out clubbing.

Her naked body was found in a small memorial park. She had been badly beaten, raped and strangled.

The murderer was still at large.

"How stupid of me. I never thought," replied Dawn.

Tony smiled grimly.

"That's normally how people become victims. They just ignore the warning signs."

Dawn regarded his handsome features.

"Well, I'm flattered you thought of me. It was very nice of you. I appreciate it."

She then looked at him.

"My name is Dawn."

"I'm Tony. Where do you live?"

"Oaktree Flats. Stokes Croft."

"Okay, I know it," replied Tony, "That's not too far. I'll make sure you get home safely."

They talked for a while. Dawn began to feel better. The cold night air seemed to help sober her up.

She found herself telling Tony about Trent.

Tony had listened. He told her that she had been unfortunate, but not to judge all men by the same book.

Dawn began to believe that he may be right. He seemed a gentleman as far as women were concerned and you didn't find many of those in this day and age.

Well, not in her life anyway.

She began to feel more optimistic.

She was enjoying Tony's company and his attention.

Maybe Christmas might hold some excitement for her after all.

As they walked on out of the city centre, it got quieter and less people were milling around.

The snow was falling a little heavier now and the traffic had died away, making things quiet and serene.

Tony looked at this phone.

"Let's take this street here," he said, "It's a shortcut according to Google Maps."

"Are you sure?" asked Dawn.

"Positive. It'll take at least 5 or 6 minutes off our journey. Trust me."

Dawn linked Tony's arm and smiled.

"Okay."

They walked in silence for a few moments. Then Dawn asked.

"So, Tony, do you have a girlfriend or maybe a wife and two kids tucked away at home?"

Tony's rugged but handsome features broke into a grin.

"The answer to that is neither. My job doesn't exactly have sociable hours for a steady relationship. Plus, working the doors makes it easy to pick up girls if I wish."

Dawn felt a slight pang of regret in her stomach.

"So, you like to play the field, is that right?"

Tony looked her in the eyes.

"Maybe I just haven't found the right girl yet for me to settle down."

Dawn smiled coyly.

"Is that right?"

With that, Tony stepped closer and lightly kissed her lips.

Dawn felt a shudder rush through her body and responded by kissing him back.

* * *

The man remained at a distance and stayed concealed in the darkness. He watched the couple kiss.

He had to wait and control his urges until he was one hundred percent sure that the time was right.

It wouldn't be long now. He sensed it.

* * *

Dawn and Tony walked on.

Dawn looked around her.

"Are you sure you took the right road? I don't recognise it."

Tony didn't answer. He was checking his phone again.

Suddenly, there was a squeal of tyres as a white transit van came around the corner and pulled up sharply by them.

The doors slid open and out jumped Chris and Errol, the other two doormen from the club.

"You found her then?" said Chris.

"Yes, I certainly did. Too good a find to let go."

Tony now gripped Dawn's arm tightly.

Dawn suddenly had a squirming feeling in her stomach.

"What's going on here?" she asked.

"Go around to the back of the van and open it up," Tony gestured to Errol.

Errol did this as Chris jumped into the driver's seat.

"Come on! Get her inside, man! Before somebody comes!"

Tony turned to Dawn and smiled.

"Now, don't struggle. It'll make things a lot easier."

Dawn felt her legs turn to jelly and all her resistance drain away.

"Please let me go. I haven't done you any harm. I don't understand. I thought you liked me and wanted to help me?"

Tony's eyes had now turned cold and dead. They reminded Dawn of a shark's eyes.

"You stupid bitch. You're all the same. Needy, spoilt, little princesses. I see them every week. Pissed up little whores flashing their asses and tits. Just asking for it. You need to be taught a lesson."

Realisation now hit Dawn like a speeding truck.

The girl who was raped and murdered. In the paper, it had said something about doormen being interviewed as the police were following up on a lead they had. They believed a doorman may be involved.

She was now sure that it was these men. It had all been a set-up. A clever, pre-meditated set-up.

Errol joined Tony as they both dragged Dawn towards the open back doors of the van.

Dawn saw a dirty double mattress laying on the van's floor and what looked like manacles drilled into the bulkhead. She tried to scream, but Tony covered her mouth with a huge hand.

Errol grinned.

"Hey, Tony! You sure picked a lively one. She's a beauty!"

"Yeah. Well, I get to go first this time. I found her," replied Tony.

Suddenly, a voice sounded from behind them.

"Let the girl go."

Both men spun around to see a man stood there.

He was clad all in black.

Black jeans and boots. Black trench coat and gloves and a black beanie pulled tightly down on his head. His face was partially obscured by the dim street lighting, but it carried a growth of beard.

Tony spoke.

"Keep walking, mister, and mind your own business."

"Yeah, keep walking," echoed Errol, "Go deliver that box of Milk Tray, brother."

He laughed at his own joke, a reference to an iconic 70s' TV advert.

The man stepped closer and spoke in a low, even voice.

"This is my business. This is what I've been sent for."

Tony smiled grimly.

"I don't know who the fuck you think you are, but…"

The man interrupted him.

"I am Michael and I am here to do God's work."

Chris now joined the other two.

"What the fuck is happening here?"

He suddenly saw the man.

"Who the fuck is this dude?"

The man spoke again.

"I am Michael and…"

This time it was Tony's turn to interrupt.

"Listen, you fucking fruitcake, you have ten seconds to piss off or you'll get badly hurt."

Tony's hand slipped into the knuckleduster inside his coat pocket as he spoke.

Errol now shoved Dawn into the back of the van. She was too petrified to offer any resistance. Her night was going from bad to worse by the minute.

The man called Michael stepped right up to Tony.

"I saw what you did to the blonde-haired guy outside the club, so I won't underestimate you. I know all about your reputation. I also know you raped and murdered Lily Baines. So, I'm asking you one more time to leave the girl and surrender to your punishment."

Tony laughed.

"You've got some balls, I'll say that for you, but you've had your warning. I have no idea what you're talking about, but you're now in a shitstorm of trouble, my friend. I'm going to fuck you up badly."

Tony shifted his weight slightly in preparation for attack. Before he could land his intended punch, the man snaked out his lead hand with blinding speed in the shape of a claw and drove it into the big man's eyes.

Tony was momentarily blinded and, within that second, it enabled the man to unclip and draw a razor-sharp tanto knife from the sheath on his trousers belt, which he drove in an icepick grip straight into Tony's neck, severing the carotid artery and jugular vein.

The man knew within minutes that death would arrive.

As the man withdrew the blade and stepped back, Tony collapsed to his knees. A spectacular eruption of blood spurted from the fatal wound. A look of surprise and horror was etched across his face.

Before Errol could react, the man sliced the blade in a reverse grip across the big black guy's windpipe. He staggered back against the van doors clutching his throat in a futile gesture, trying to stem the tide of crimson.

Chris had seen enough and ran for the front door and sanctuary of the driver's cab. He might have made it, only his flailing jacket caught on one of the wing mirrors, which slowed him down. Long enough for the man in black to be on him in the blink of an eye.

Chris screamed out in excruciating pain as the knife was thrust up his anus. Retracting the blade, it now penetrated his left kidney.

Chris sagged to his knees.

With cold detachment, the man pulled Chris's head back by hooking his fingers into his nostrils and then drove the blade icepick fashion into the suprasternal notch at the base of the throat. He wiped the blade clean on the dead man's jacket and returned it to its sheath.

Regarding the bodies, he spoke.

"May God forgive you all. I deliver your souls for judgement."

The execution was over in a few minutes. It had been clinically delivered by somebody who knew exactly what they were doing.

The man named Michael walked to the back of the van. He regarded the girl curled up in the corner sobbing.

She flinched away from him and buried her face in her hands.

She was shaking like a leaf.

"Please don't kill me," she whimpered.

Dawn couldn't look up at the man. She was paralysed with fear. She kept her head lowered in the mattress that filled the floor of the van.

The man spoke.

"You have nothing to fear. It's over. I have no agenda to harm you. You are free to go. Those three men were sinners and they needed to be punished. They will never hurt you again or anybody else. I've been watching them for some time now and waiting for the perfect moment to execute my redemption. Tonight, it came. I was given a sign. God will now decide their final fate when their souls leave this earth. Go now before the police arrive. Forget what happened here tonight. Go home and give thanks for your deliverance to safety from the devil's followers. Learn from this and change your ways."

"Who are you?" asked Dawn.

"I am Michael," came the reply, "I am a soldier of the Lord."

When Dawn finally found the courage to look up, the man was no longer there.

Chapter 2

DCI Harry Bowe was woken from his sleep by the sound of his mobile phone pinging. He reached out in the darkness and retrieved it from the bedside table. Next to him, his wife Carol stirred.

Bowe looked at the screen. It was a text from DS Diane Rose.

It read: *Sorry to disturb you Sir but please ring me urgently.*

He pulled back the bed covers and took the phone to the bathroom so as not to disturb Carol any further. He knew that she had to be up bright and early for her shift at the hospital.

The police force and indeed the NHS did not ever stop working.

Bowe shut the bathroom door and switched on the light. He momentarily regarded his tired features in the mirror. This job would be the death of him.

He rang DS Rose.

From experience, he knew that receiving a call in the wee small hours of the morning didn't bode well. Twenty years in the police force prepared you for these occasions, but there was always a tingle of adrenaline in the belly as you made the call.

DC Rose answered it after one ring.

"Hello, sir. Sorry to wake you, but I think you need to hear this."

Harry's senses immediately heightened. He was now wide awake.

"Go on, Diane. What have you got?"

"Looks like he's struck again. Three dead. A right bloodbath. The victims were known to us. We had them in the frame for the recent rape and murder of Lily Baines in the downtown area. The three doormen. Tony Ellis, Chris Comer and Errol White who worked at the Jungle Club in the city centre. These men, as you know, were handy, to say the least, but somebody has gone through them like they were nothing. All have died from knife wounds."

"Christ!" exclaimed Harry, "You sure it wasn't some sort of altercation that carried on over outside the club?"

Diane Rose explained her reasons for her deduction that it wasn't the case.

Harry took in the information.

In recent months, there had been two other unusual murders in Bristol.

The first was the murder of a convicted paedophile, Roger Hunt, who had been released early from prison after the powers-to-be authorised him fit to rejoin society. He had only been out for a few weeks when he had been seen outside a primary school a few miles from where he lived. The police had issued him a severe warning that he was breaking the terms of his probation. If he did it again, he would be back inside.

That night, somebody had visited his bedsit and slit his throat after first castrating him. Not a pleasant way to go.

The bedsit he was staying in was only known to a handful of people in the police and social services. How his killer knew his whereabouts was a mystery at present.

The other murder had been of Dale Hicks, local pimp and all-round nasty piece of work. His body had been discovered in a dumpster at the back of a fast-food restaurant. He had died from a long, thin blade being inserted through the base of his skull and up into his brain.

The day before, Hicks had been in court on a drugs charge. He was acquitted on a technicality and released. He gloated to the police on the steps of the courthouse that they had nothing on him. Next night, he was found dead.

Both murders were certainly gruesome, but both held the hallmarks of somebody detached and methodical. They had not been frenzied attacks, but very much organised and calculated.

Neither victim showed any defensive wounds on their hands or arms. They hadn't seen the attack coming.

Examination of the bodies by a forensic pathologist suggested that, due to their ferocity, the attacks were probably executed by a male. A left-handed and strong male. The evidence present also revealed that the perpetrator of these crimes was skilled and trained.

Due to the manner of the killings, they were most certainly premeditated. These men had been hunted down and ruthlessly dispatched.

DCI Bowe had been assigned to the case and was told in no uncertain terms by his Chief Superintendent Andrew Bradley that he needed to catch this killer fast.

Up to now, they had no leads or any DNA evidence of any significant worth.

Now armed with the information of this latest murder, Harry knew only too well that all the victims had been criminals and on the wrong side of the law.

None of their deaths would be particularly mourned in policing circles, that was for sure, but the alarming thought was that there might be a vigilante on the prowl. That was disturbing.

"Give me the address and I'm on my way," said Bowe.

Ten minutes later, DCI Harry Bowe was in his car and on his way to the scene of the murder.

Bowe was a hardened veteran of the homicide division in Bristol and had seen just about every atrocity that one human being could do to another. He was known as a tough boss, but a fair one. That said, nobody in the squad wanted to get on the wrong side of him.

Harry was well aware of the fact that, when hearing his name for the first time, everyone thought of Haribo – the well-known brand of top-selling children's sweets – but they wisely never mentioned it. Well, not to his face.

The DCI was 50 years of age. He was an athletic 88kg and stood 6'. He was a regular gym user and a black belt in Judo from his younger days.

He could handle himself well enough in a bad situation. He also had a sharp policeman's brain and a dry sense of humour, which surfaced occasionally.

He was born in Bristol, but did the majority of his policing in the Midlands, Birmingham and Coventry mostly, before being stationed back to the city of his birth.

He had been married to his wife Carol for five years. She was a nurse. This was his second marriage. His first produced two children, James and Holly, both now grown up. One was living in Jersey and one in the States. He kept in touch when he could, but they mostly led their own lives. When they were growing up, Harry had been too immersed in his job to give them much time. His then-wife Layla had borne all the responsibility of parenting and this had ultimately led to their break-up once the children were old enough to fend for themselves.

He had met Carol at A&E where she had been working. He had accompanied the paramedics into hospital with a suspect. A burglar who had been stabbed by the owner of the house he had broken into.

Carol and Harry had shared some conversations during his wait to see if the man survived major surgery. There had been an instant attraction between them and before the end of the night when Harry knew that his suspect had come through surgery, he sought out Carol and asked if she would like to go for a drink with him sometime.

That was the start of their relationship.

Carol had lost her first husband to cancer and had been on her own ever since. Like Harry, she lived for her job as a nurse.

They were both career driven people, but this was why their relationship worked because they didn't put demands on each other and both understood the pressures of their jobs and how much they meant to them.

Five years down the line, they were both happy and comfortable in their relationship.

* * *

It took Harry twenty-five minutes to reach the address DS Rose had given him. As he pulled up to the crime scene, he saw lights had been put up and SOCO were swarming around like ants.

DS Rose spotted his car and walked over towards it. She was clad in crime scene overalls.

Diane Rose was an experienced copper. Bright, tough and ambitious. She was 34 years of old, unmarried and not in any current relationship. She was an attractive blonde with a soft side that she rarely showed at work. Harry worked well with her.

Harry pulled his stiff frame out of the car and nodded to Diane. He had been to the gym earlier that evening and he wasn't sure at his age whether to do more exercise or give it up altogether.

The night was bitterly cold, but at least the earlier snow hadn't amounted to anything.

"Hello, sir. Sorry to spoil your night off," she said.

"No worries, Diane. We're never really off the job, are we?"

Diane smiled.

"I guess not."

Harry looked around.

"So, we think it's our boy again, do we?"

"It all points that way, sir."

"Well, we better take a look then."

Harry went to the boot of his car and retrieved his own scene overalls, gloves and overshoes. Then, they both headed to the murder site, which was cordoned off with police tape.

Harry recognised Constable Rob Bailey standing watch. Bailey was a young, up-and-coming policeman who Harry liked. As the young man saw DCI Bowe approaching, he straightened up.

"Evening, sir."

Harry nodded.

"Evening, Bailey. Did you discover the bodies?"

"No, sir. The couple over there with the paramedics came across them, but I was the first officer on the scene along with Constable Sharma. The station received a phone message from said couple informing them of the murder. We were in the area and got the call and came here and secured the scene."

"You did well, son. Go get yourself a cup of tea and warm up for a while. We've got things here for now," replied Harry, "Where's Sharma?"

Constable DC Mira Sharma was another young and capable copper. Born in Bristol but of Asian heritage, she was proving a valuable asset to the force.

"She's on the far side of the perimeter, sir."

"Make sure you grab her a hot drink as well."

"I will, sir. Thank you."

* * *

Harry and Diane both ducked under the tape and walked towards an abandoned white Ford Transit.

"Have we run the plate?" asked Harry.

"Yes, sir. The van is registered to one of the deceased, Errol White."

The back doors of the van were open and SOCO were working in and around it. The bodies lay on the ground covered in sheets.

Harry spied forensic pathologist Doctor Brendan Daly. Daly was of Irish descent. He was a big man with thinning red hair and a matching bushy beard. He was in his late fifties and was a veteran of his trade.

"What have we got, Brendan?"

The big man turned around.

"Hello, Harry. I thought this might be yours. We have a slaughterhouse here. That's what we have."

Brendan nodded to two of his assistants and they pulled back the covers on the bodies. Harry and Diane moved closer to them, along with the pathologist.

"All killed with a knife of some sort. Possible six inches or longer. No sign of the murder weapon present."

Brendan pointed at the bodies individually.

"This one was stabbed in the neck, severing the carotid artery. This one had his throat slashed wide open. This one looks like he was trying to run away, but was caught. He was stabbed in the anus, then the left kidney and finally in the suprasternal notch."

"The where'?" asked Diane Rose.

Brendan pointed to the indentation at the base of his throat.

"So, this wasn't some fight or feud then?" asked Harry.

"No," replied Brendan, "These guys have no defensive wounds on their hands. They didn't get a chance to fight back. Whoever did this did it very efficiently with speed and accuracy."

Harry thought back to the evidence of the other two recent killings. The similarities were all there to be seen.

"Do you know if the killer was left or right-handed?"

Brendan stroked his beard, always a sign that he was contemplating an accurate answer. He wasn't a man of random assumptions.

"I will need to study the bodies more closely to be 100% sure, but on preliminary investigation, I would say left-handed."

Bowe and Rose exchanged glances.

The killer of Hunt and Hicks had been left-handed.

Harry inspected the corpses more closely. He recognised the men immediately. It was only a week previously that he had interviewed them at the Jungle Club.

"These men were on our radar for a serious crime and were known to us. Three months ago, a 23-year-old girl was raped and strangled after leaving the club. An anonymous tipoff to the police suggested the three men were the perpetrators," he told Daly.

Harry knew that they all had previous for violence. All were veteran door personnel who knew the nightclub scene well. They also pumped iron and boxed at the Vault Gym. The place was full of power-lifting monsters and bodybuilders. It was also known for illegal drug use and other dodgy activities.

"These boys could have a row and look after themselves. Whoever did this has got to have specialised training," said Harry.

"I would tend to agree with that assumption, Harry," said Brendan Daly.

"Time of death?" asked Harry.

"Again, this is not wholly accurate, but as a rough guess and from their present body composition, I would say they've been dead a few hours, but the cold temperature might have altered that slightly. I'll know more when I've conducted the autopsies."

"Okay. Thanks, Brendan. I'll be in touch."

DCI Bowe now turned to Diane.

"The witnesses?"

Diane consulted her notebook.

"Terry and Emily Frost. Married. They were walking back from a friend's party and came across the scene.

There was nobody here, except the three dead men and the van. They called it straight in. Both are in shock and Mrs Frost is feeling faint and nauseous. The paramedics are looking after them."

"CCTV?" asked Harry, scanning the surroundings.

"No, sir. No cameras on this stretch. It's pretty isolated. That may have been planned."

"Footprints?"

"Nothing of worth," said Rose, "It snowed pretty continuously for a while since the incident and it covered the scene. If there had been any footprints of note, they're now gone."

Harry walked to the back of the van and looked inside. It was empty, except for a large, stained mattress in the back. He also instantly saw the manacles.

On the ground in sealed plastic evidence bags were a roll of duct tape, cable ties, rope and handcuffs. From past experience, it looked 100% like a rape kit to Harry.

"So, what do you think happened? Did the killer follow them and catch them cold or did they pick up an intended victim and the killer intervened?"

DS Rose spread her arms and shrugged.

"Could have been either. I don't believe the killer came across them by chance though. I think he must have been watching them and planning this."

"How would he know they were suspected rapists and murderers in the first place? That was only known to us," replied Harry.

DS Rose shook her head.

"That I don't know, sir. Maybe he just came across them by chance?"

"And like every good citizen, stabbed them to death and didn't report it?" replied Harry.

DS Rose smiled.

"You have a point, sir."

Harry looked back towards the three bodies now being moved to the coroner's van.

"If these men had picked up another potential victim, where are they and why didn't they contact us?"

"Scared maybe. Especially if she witnessed these killings with her own eyes. Extreme trauma can make people react in strange ways."

DCI Bowe said nothing.

With these three men now dead, it would be impossible to prove they raped and murdered 23-year-old Lily Baines. There would be no closure to the case for the victim's parents unless this other intended victim came forward.

Some would argue that the men would not be missed and got what they deserved. Somebody had saved the taxpayer a lot of money.

That person had decided to take out their own retribution on these men, as well as the previous two lowlifes. They also didn't attempt to conceal their crimes. The bodies were left for all to see.

A message?

Harry felt a shiver run up his spine and he knew that it wasn't due to the chill of this winter's night.

Somebody dangerous was lurking out there on the streets and it was his job to find them. They had killed on three occasions so far and had left no evidence behind and nobody had seen or heard a thing.

This man was a ghost. A shadow.

DCI Harry Bowe knew with every fibre of his being that this would not be the man's last kill. He was getting a taste for it now and enjoying it.

The city couldn't afford a 'caped crusader' bumping off criminals. Before you knew it, you'd have complete anarchy. People would be murdered for using their mobile phone whilst driving or gunned down for running a red light. Where do you draw the line?

Chapter 3

The next morning at 9:00am sharp, DCI Bowe stood in the incident room at Temple Police Headquarters, Bristol. His investigating team were also all there.

Behind Bowe was a large murder board with the images of the deceased in this investigation.

Harry took a sip of his coffee. It was wet and warm, but that was all its redeeming features.

He now addressed the assembled room.

"We had three more murders in the early hours of this morning and from the evidence present, we believe the same person is responsible for these as the murders of Roger Hunt and Dale Hicks."

"So, it's 'The Ghost' then?" commented DS James Leech between chomps on his bacon sandwich.

Leech was an experienced copper and had been around the block a few times. He was in his mid-forties and exhibited all the signs of a stereotypical, middle-aged male. Overweight, receding hairline and unkempt appearance.

He wasn't always politically correct or in tune with today's modern trends, but he was dogged and determined when he got his teeth stuck into a case. Bowe was glad to have him as part of his team even if he had to rein him in from time to time.

Harry didn't like the name 'Ghost', but this is what the tabloids and media had started calling the killer, which was all down to Tommy Good, or 'Goodie' as he was known. He was the editor of the local newspaper, *The Bristol Eye*.

Harry had a tolerating working relationship with the man who sometimes could be a pain in the ass when going off on his own crusade for justice.

"Yes, Jim. It's almost certainly our man."

Harry looked towards DS Rose.

"DS Rose will now fill you in on the details of the recent murders. She was the first senior officer on the scene."

Diane Rose explained what she had found, who the victims were and the method of the killings.

"So, nobody saw anything at all. Nothing suspicious?" asked DS Carrie French.

Carrie was relatively new to the team, having transferred from Oxford. She was a red head. Her trademark was her extensive collection of designer glasses. Today she sported an impressive pair of purple ones that would have made Sir Elton John envious. She was a whizz in trawling and finding evidence in the police archives.

"Nothing, Carrie. The witnesses who discovered the bodies came across them well after the incident and there was no CCTV in the area. If there was another intended victim, they disappeared from the scene unnoticed," replied DS Rose.

Constable Rob Bailey chipped in.

"DC Sharma and I tracked back along the route the van may have taken and spoke to some of the late-night revellers, but to be honest, most of them wouldn't have been capable of taking anything in, even if it happened in front of their noses."

There was a chuckle around the room.

"I'm going to put out a press release later and appeal to anybody around that clubland area if they saw anything suspicious and plead directly to a possible intended victim," said Harry, "We spoke with the manager of the Jungle Club, Terry Stone, and he told me that the three deceased had worked on the door that night and it just seemed to be a night like any other. There were a few disturbances, but nothing of note to suggest what had happened to them later. He was shocked that these men had been murdered.

"So, we can definitely rule out that it isn't a work incident and a disgruntled punter looking for payback?" asked Leech.

"If you were a drunk punter coming back for a touch of revenge against these men, you would have had to bring a Magnum 44 with you," replied Harry.

Again, there was a chuckle around the room.

"This didn't put our killer off though, did it?" replied Carrie French.

There was now a moment of silence reflecting on this comment.

"As we expected then, this looks like somebody is bumping off some of the dregs of our society," said Leech.

Harry tried to steer the question away from the suggestion of a vigilante being out on the streets.

"We can't be 100% sure of that, Jim, so we've got to keep this lowkey for the minute. Otherwise, the press and the public are gonna have a field day with it."

Carrie French spoke again.

"With respect, sir, it'll be hard to keep a lid on this. All the evidence is pointing in favour of a vigilante."

"That may be so, Sergeant French, but that word is not to be uttered outside of these four walls for now. Is that understood? That goes for all of you. I don't want this lunatic ending up a public darling. Regardless who he's murdered, he's committed crimes that he needs to answer for. Understand?"

Carrie French nodded, suitably chastised by her boss.

"Sir?"

Harry regarded Constable Kenny Stewart.

Stewart was also new to the team. He had come down from Glasgow. His thick accent sometimes made it difficult for his colleagues to understand him. He was a tough lad and had seen his share of action on the streets.

"Yes, Kenny?" replied Harry.

If, as you say, it is 'The Ghost' and he's bumping off society's lowlifes, what had these last three men done to fall into that category?"

Harry filled Kenny in on the details.

"We recently received information that these men may well have been involved in the rape and murder of a girl named Lily Baines, last seen leaving the Jungle Club and briefly speaking to the three doormen on the way out. This all occurred over the last three months. We've been piecing a case together to bring to the CPS."

"How then did 'The Ghost' know about them, sir?"

Harry took another sip of his coffee. It hadn't improved.

"That I don't know, Kenny."

Leech spoke up again.

"The other two victims had recently been mentioned in the local rag, *The Bristol Eye*, so our boy probably got his information from there and did a bit of tracking himself."

"Maybe, but it still doesn't explain how he knew about the latest three," replied Harry.

The DCI now addressed the room.

"Any update in relation to the other murders?"

Sergeant Leech answered.

"Nothing, guv. No witnesses and no DNA left at the crime scene. Both victims were taken out before they knew anything about it. These are not, as we suspect, random killings. They were targeted. Hunt in his flat. The front door was just kicked in and the killer entered and quickly dispatched the bastard in his bed. Dale Hicks was walking back to his car from picking up a late-night Big Mac and fries when he was attacked. It was fast and vicious."

"McDonald's didn't make his day then," quipped DC Bailey.

A ripple of laughter went around the room.

Leech continued.

"Again, Hicks was no pushover when it came to dishing out violence, but he was obliterated."

Harry nodded.

"Thanks, Jim."

He now looked around the room.

"Somebody, somewhere must know something. This person can't just vanish into thin air. Keep looking, keep probing. Follow up phone calls or leads. You know the drill. We'll meet up at 4:00pm tomorrow afternoon for the latest updates. We have to try and catch this man before he kills again."

"You think he will?" asked Carrie French.

Harry regarded her.

"Yes, I do. I think he's just getting into his stride and if he's targeting criminals in this city, he has a vast melting pot of filth to choose from."

Harry now regarded DS Leech.

"Jim, I want you and DC Bailey to go back to the Jungle Club, get the manager Stone to pull up Sunday morning's CCTV footage. Let's see if anybody turns up on there who might be of interest. It's worth a look."

"Will do, sir," replied Leech.

"Sir, I have some news."

It was Sergeant Ali Khan, another dependable member of the team. Khan had done most of his policing on the streets of Birmingham and that's how he had got to know Harry. DCI Bowe had been responsible for getting him a transfer when he came back to Bristol himself.

"Yes, Ali. What have you got?"

"News from SOCO, sir. In the examination of the victim's van, they came across a bracelet in the back under a mattress. It had an engraving on the inner side reading *To Dawn, Love Trent*. They're running it through tests now to see if there's any DNA on it. If so, they'll put it through the database."

"Great," replied Harry, "Get them to send through some images of it. I'll get them out with the press release and also make sure other media sources get them as well. The owner of that bracelet might have been the latest target and may have witnessed everything. We need to find this Dawn fast. Okay, everybody! That's it for now."

As the team disbursed, Harry's phone pinged.

He looked at the screen.

Shit, it was a text from Superintendent Bradley.

The message read: *I need to see you urgently*.

Harry pocketed his phone and looked at DS Rose.

"Diane, I have to see the old man. Keep an eye on things here and set up that press release with Goodie for me, will you?"

"I'm on it, sir," replied Rose.

* * *

As Harry took the lift to the second floor, he considered the bracelet. There was no evidence yet that it could belong to another intended victim of the rapists, but there just might be a chance that they had picked up another girl and were ready to drive her off when their killer appeared. It was the best lead they had to go on, so he would take it.

As he exited the lift and walked down the corridor towards the Superintendent's office, he prayed that this was the right deduction. He needed something positive to give to Bradley to pacify him for the moment and keep him off his back.

Chapter 4

Harry knocked on the Superintendent's office door and heard a voice from beyond say, "Come in."

Harry opened the door and walked into a modern, spacious office. All glass and polished wood. Behind a large desk in front of a picture window that gave a great view of the city sat Andrew Bradley.

He was in his mid-fifties. A smart man, trim and fit. He had steel grey hair and a neat beard and moustache to match. He had served his time in the force, working his way up through the police ranks to his present position.

He had only been in this job a year following the previous superintendent's retirement. The job had almost been a certainty for Andrew Bradley. His police record was exemplary.

He was a no-nonsense, tough individual. He was no pencil-pushing desk jockey. He had seen and done his fair share of hands-on policing over the years. Harry respected that.

Bradley gestured to a seat in front of his desk.

"Sit down, Harry."

Harry pulled up a chair.

"Bring me up to speed with the latest on the case."

Over the next ten minutes, Harry filled Bradley in on the latest developments. The Superintendent listened intently and at no time interrupted him.

When Harry had finished, Bradley sat back in his chair looking thoughtful.

"The finding of the bracelet could be a breakthrough."

Harry nodded.

"We hope so, sir."

"Have you any idea how this killer knew about the three doormen? The other two victims are more understandable. Hunt had been all over the local papers and media when he was released from prison. This person could have just simply followed him on his release to his flat. Hicks was a well-known pimp in the area. It wouldn't have been too hard to track him down. But the others... we were only beginning to build a case against them. Nobody else could have known. Did any member of your team let it slip to anybody?"

Harry shook his head.

"Absolutely not."

"You're sure?"

"Yes, sir. 100%."

"Okay, Harry. On top of all that's going on, we don't want a snitch amongst our ranks."

"I'm sure that's not the case," answered Harry.

Bradley seemed to be pacified.

"Do you think he'll strike again?"

Harry leant forward in his chair.

"Yes, sir. I do. As yet, there seems to be no pattern to these killings. As far as we can ascertain, the victims didn't know each other. The killings seem random. That's why it's so difficult to deduce where he'll strike next."

"Well, let's hope the bracelet brings us some joy."

"Is that all, sir?" said Harry, rising from his seat.

"Yes. But keep me up to speed with any new developments."

Harry nodded and headed for the door.

"Oh Harry…" called Bradley, "Commissioner Harper and Mayor Barnes are crawling up my ass on this matter. They're worried about mass hysteria if the press prints anything about a lunatic out on the streets randomly killing people. We can't have that at any costs. The police are not exactly flavour of the month with the public at present. Three killings in our city in as many months cannot be tolerated. Nail this fucker sooner rather than later. Okay?"

Harry opened the door.

"Understood, sir."

* * *

When Harry got back to his office, DS Rose was waiting for him.

"Tommy Good will see you at 1:00pm today at *The Bristol Eye*'s offices."

"Thanks," replied Harry.

"Sir, I had a thought about how the killer might have known about the three doormen," said Rose.

Harry perched on the edge of a desk.

"Go on, Diane. I'm listening."

"Well, these guys were all tight. If you commit a crime of this serious nature as we suspected they did, you would all stick together. Swear each other to secrecy."

"Yes, I agree," intervened Harry.

Diane continued.

"But somewhere, you would like to brag about it or relive the memory."

"Where are we heading with this, Diane?" asked Harry.

"We know they were all regulars at the Vault Gym. A place that isn't exactly David Lloyds. A lot of ex-cons and people of interest go there. It would be a perfect place for them to discuss their deed between themselves and plan for another. Maybe in the changing rooms or sauna.

"Go on," said Harry.

"Suppose our killer uses the gym and overheard a conversation they had and learnt that they killed off Lily Baines."

Harry regarded Diane.

"It's a long shot, but it's worth looking into. Maybe the killer recently joined the gym. They might have membership. A name. A face. It's worth a visit."

"I'm up for that, sir."

Diane saw a flicker of concern cross her boss's face.

"What's the matter, Harry? Think a woman isn't up to going into a place like the Vault?'

Harry smiled.

"Maybe some women, but I got a feeling you'll be okay. Take Constable Stewart with you for company."

"Will do, sir. I'll get on it now."

Harry watched Diane go. He knew she could look after herself, but a place like the Vault Gym was no holiday camp. He would be happier if Kenny Stewart went with her. Apparently, he was a decent kickboxer. Hopefully, he wouldn't have to use his skills.

Chapter 5

The man called Michael awoke with a start. The nightmares had come again. Although the air in the room was chilly, his body was bathed in a thin sheen of sweat.

The images were still vivid in his mind, even after all this time. The professionals had told him that the images may never fade.

Daylight was streaming through the small window in the room where he slept. He threw back the blankets and sat up on the edge of the camp bed. He waited for the trembling to subside in his limbs.

His thoughts now went to earlier this morning and the killings. He was satisfied that the evil had been eradicated. As a spiritual warrior, he had escorted these bad men into the afterlife where they would be judged. God or Lucifer would decide their fate now, not the law.

The law was weak and rotten from the inside out. It allowed sinners to walk free with little or no punishment. Prisons didn't deter individuals from reoffending, nor did it rehabilitate them. Society had gone soft, and scum were free to roam and inflict pain and suffering to innocent people without any recompense.

God must look down on the world he had created and weep. As almighty as he was, he needed help and support. That's why he had called upon Michael to help do his work. He needed a man of certain skills to do his bidding.

Michael was that man.

An eye for an eye. A tooth for a tooth.

He looked around the sparse room. It was cold in there. His body had begun to cool.

He got up, went over to a small electric heater and switched it on. The warmth soon came out of it, but you only really felt the heat if you sat a foot away.

Michael headed to the bathroom, which was located off the main room. Returning to the living area, he now filled a kettle from a small sink and plugged it in. He spooned coffee into a mug and added some long-life milk to it. As he waited for the kettle to boil, he dressed.

His clothes were cold as he put them on. *Never mind*, he thought. He had been in worse conditions. He had endured many discomforts in his life.

The room was austere, but it was free and also well concealed. He felt safe here.

Michael heard footsteps above his head. Somebody was moving around.

He checked his watch. It read 10:15am. He hadn't intended to sleep that long, but it had been 3:30am this morning when he had crawled into bed.

The kettle clicked off and Michael made his coffee. As he sipped it, he looked out of the window. There wasn't much to see: just the back of another building and a small patch of grass.

Suddenly, a bird landed on the grass and began pecking at the frozen ground. Michael recognised the bird as a thrush. The bird was obviously hungry, but the hard ground was making it difficult to find food.

Michael opened a small cupboard and brought out half a loaf of bread. He broke some off and then quietly opened the window and threw it out onto the grass. Within seconds, the thrush had hopped over to it and started pecking away.

Michael smiled.

He then recalled a Bible quote. Job 12:10. *"In God's hand is the soul of every creature and the breath of all mankind."*

How true.

Suddenly, a bell began to peel and the bird took flight.

Michael finished his coffee.

He needed to buy some food supplies. He was running low.

He would be here for a while yet. He still had souls to deliver.

Putting on his coat, hat and gloves, he unlocked the door of his room. A chilly blast of cold air hit him in the face and a smell of dampness assaulted his nostrils. He headed up the winding stone steps to up above and the way out.

As he ascended, the peeling of the bells grew louder. At the top of the stairs, he opened another door and stepped into chapel area of St Mathias Church. There, he spied Father Matthew Munroe, who was the priest of the parish.

Father Matthew looked up from lighting a candle. He was in his mid-sixties. He was a rotund man with a ruddy complexion due to many years preaching down in Cornwall at a small parish that he once ran right next to the sea. It could also be put down to his partial fondness for malt whisky.

"Good morning, Michael. I trust you slept well. Sorry it's so cold downstairs. The church this time of year is a draughty place, unfortunately."

"Good morning, Father. The cold is bearable. I'm on my way to get some breakfast, then I need to buy some groceries."

"You missed 8:00am mass this morning. Unusual for you," said Father Matthew.

"I'm sorry. I slept right through. Late night last night."

Father Matthew smiled. He knew better than to pry.

"No matter. Maybe you'll attend evening mass at 6:00pm instead."

"Yes, maybe I will," replied Michael.

Father Matthew began to burn incense and spread it around the altar by swinging a thurible.

The smell made Michael recall a time long ago when he was a young boy and attended church with his parents. They had both been devout Catholics. This memory seemed like it was from another lifetime. He wondered what they would think of him now and the life he had chosen.

Michael moved closer to the smoke of the incense and breathed it in. For a moment, he was a child again. Carefree and happy.

"Are you alright, Michael?" asked Father Matthew.

Michael opened his eyes, the visions evaporated.

"I'm fine. I'll see you later, Father."

Michael walked over to the side door by the altar and let himself out into the chilly morning air. He began to walk over to his black transit van. He had bought it for next to nothing from an old army buddy a few weeks ago. It wasn't great, but it would do to get him about the city. The motorway was another matter.

A few early parishioners were heading to the church for the 11:00am service.

He pulled his coat collar up and put his head down. As he walked, he thought about Father Matthew.

Michael had come to Bristol three months ago. He had been born and bred here, before leaving a long time ago. He had been living abroad up until recently when he decided that it was time to come home to put to bed some issues.

Michael had lived wherever he could and took work wherever he could. He had no attachments and no place that he could truly call home, although Bristol was the next best thing.

He was alone in the world, but he didn't mind. He now had God as a friend and mentor.

That had not always been the case. He had not been a religious man in any shape or form until the incident that changed his life forever.

* * *

The night he arrived in Bristol, it was pouring with rain. Great Britain was in the grips of Storm Mary. She was being a right bitch with driving rain and 60mph gusts of wind.

He had hitchhiked for a lift from London with a lorry driver. He didn't want to be traced by using public transport.

Walking the streets looking for shelter, he had come across St Mathias Church and was drawn to it. He remembered, as a young boy, his father telling him that if you're in a strange place with nowhere to go, seek out a church. There will always be a welcome there. Michael took this piece of advice on board.

Surprisingly, he found the church open. He went inside, sat in a pew and tried to dry off. He was shivering with the cold and his belly rumbled with hunger. He must have gone to sleep as he was awoken by a hand gently shaking him.

It was Father Matthew.

The priest had asked Michael if he was homeless to which he had replied yes.

The storm was terrible, so he brought the younger man back to his rectory and made him some hot soup. He then brought out the whisky bottle.

They talked long into the night.

In his younger years, Father Matthew had been an army chaplain and he sensed that the man sat by the fire in front of him was from a military background. He could see that he had hit hard times and society had cast him aside as it did to so many of its ex-soldiers. This man's face bore the scars of somebody who had seen the darker side of life.

Michael had confessed to the priest that he had been in the forces, but didn't expand upon it. Father Matthew didn't push the matter as he saw it was tough for Michael to speak about it. He felt sorry for the younger man.

He knew if the man wanted to speak more about his experiences in the forces, he would do it in his own time.

The priest told Michael that he did have a small room empty in the church crypt. He often let people down on their luck use it. He offered Michael the room rent free if he would turn his hand to odd jobs around the church and the grounds. The parish council would also be able to offer a small wage.

Michael was truly grateful and accepted the offer. For the last three months, he had been living with a roof over his head and food in his belly.

He got on well with Father Matthew. On occasions, he would get an invite to the rectory for a proper sit-down supper, which he relished.

The priest never pressured him about his life or his past, which he was grateful for. Not everybody would understand his calling and what he had to do.

Michael was humbled to be living in the house of God, which seemed fitting for his mission.

He now climbed into the van, started it up and headed off to the local 7/11. The traffic was light and the roads quite clear, but he kept to the speed limit as he didn't want to get pulled over by the police.

The van wasn't insured and his license had expired a long time ago. The plates were false. He had no ID on him. To all intents and purposes, he didn't exist.

He was a ghost.

Chapter 6

DCI Harry Bowe sat in the cluttered office of Tommy 'Goodie' Good, *The Bristol Eye*'s editor.

Good was in his mid-forties. He sported a trendy goatee and had a shaven head. Both his ears were pierced copious times and he also had a nose stud.

He was a new breed of newspaper editor.

Tommy Good was a vegan and didn't touch alcohol. He was proudly gay. He was charismatic and believed himself trendy and hip with his finger on the pulse of all that was happening in the city he loved and called home. He felt it was only a matter of time before one of the leading tabloids would eventually snap him up. He lived for that day.

Harry had brought him up to speed on the latest developments, including the bracelet. SOCO had sent over images of the bracelet to Harry's phone, but after running DNA through the system, they had not come up with a hit. No criminal record was found.

"Right, Harry," said Goodie, "I'll get these images out on the front of the paper for tomorrow. Hopefully, somebody will recognise it and the engraving and come forward."

"Okay, Goodie. The sooner the better."

Harry paused for a second and then spoke.

"Have you heard anything different to what I've told you?"

Goodie shook his head.

"Shit. No, Harry. The word out there is nobody has seen or heard anything. Plus, due to the nature of the deceased, most people don't really give a shit. There are a few rumblings that Joe Public supports the killer."

"Bollocks. That's all we need. We don't want this bastard to have a fan club," exclaimed Harry.

"With all due respect, Harry, you can see why the public would not be lamenting over the deaths of these lowlifes. This killer is doing what the public think the police should have done," Goodie pointed out.

Harry glared at the man. He knew what Goodie had said had a ring of truth to it.

"The justice system grinds slowly, but it is fair."

"Maybe, Harry, but people in the city have run out of patience. They see no evidence of policing crime on the streets. Police are not making their presence felt unless they're dancing at a Pride march or the St Paul's Carnival. The biggest police presence you will see is at a fucking football match.

The 'Bobby' on the beat is non-existent. They're now sat at a desk behind a computer screen with a stack of paperwork. The community police are barely out of fucking nappies. Most couldn't fight sleep. Every week in the tabloids, we're also getting stories about rogue cops abusing their positions and committing unspeakable crimes. The public are beginning to believe every other copper is a rapist or as bent as a Yuri Geller spoon. This isn't the present climate for a police friendly atmosphere. Whoever this person is, they're taking the law into their own hands and dishing out their own form of justice."

"Alright, Goodie. You've made your point, but for now refrain from mentioning 'vigilante'. Give me a bit of breathing space to see where this bracelet takes us. Understood?" said Harry.

Goodie sighed.

"For now, Harry, okay. But the public deserves to know the truth, so I'm not going to hold back forever."

Harry stood up.

"Okay. Let's see what the next few days bring."

Goodie nodded.

"Okay. But if this guy strikes again, then I'm going public with the vigilante angle."

Harry didn't reply as he left the office.

* * *

DS Rose and PC Stewart pulled up outside the Vault Gym. It was situated on a small trading estate and the building was sandwiched between an Albanian car valeting business and a tyre fitting garage.

Both police officers got out of the car and walked over towards the building.

"So, what are we looking out for?" asked PC Stewart.

"It's a long shot, but if we can get information on anybody who has joined the gym in the last three months, we might just have a suspect among them. At least we would have some faces and names to look into. At the moment, we have nothing," answered DS Rose.

They entered the gym.

Immediately, they came to a reception area. Behind the counter was a young woman scrawling through her phone with perfectly manicured nails. She looked up as they approached the desk.

DS Rose estimated that she was probably in her early twenties. She looked like many girls of her age. Her hair was scraped back from her face and fashioned into a ponytail. She had false eyelashes, an orange sunbed tan, trout lips and breast implants.

Very *Love Island*.

She wore a tight vest top that accentuated her ample charms. Her bare arms showed off an array of interesting tattoos.

"Can I help you?" she asked in a thick Bristolian accent.

DS Rose showed her ID.

"I'm DS Rose and this is PC Stewart. Is the owner of the gym, Mr Ed Lyons, around?"

The girl studied them both as if they were aliens and then answered.

"No. I'm afraid he's out."

"And you are?" asked Rose.

"I'm his daughter, Zoe Lyons."

"Do you work here?"

"Only at weekends. I help out around the gym and do a bit of reception work."

"When will your father be back?"

"Not until tomorrow. He's gone to the football up in Sunderland. City are playing them today."

DS Rose looked around the reception and nodded.

"Zoe... can I call you Zoe?"

"Sure," replied the girl.

"Do you keep membership records of the people that train here?"

"Yeah, I guess."

"You don't sound too sure, Zoe," queried Rose.

"Well, my dad deals with all that."

"So, you wouldn't know where he keeps them?"

Just then, a big man came out from the gym. His grey t-shirt was patchy with sweat and had a job to contain his bulging muscles. He eyed the police officers suspiciously.

"Everything alright here, Zoe?"

The girl regarded the man.

"This is the police. They're asking about our members and want to see their details."

"Do they now?"

"Who are you, sir?" asked DS Rose.

The man regarded her.

"I'm Arnold Schwarzenegger. Who are you?"

"DS Rose and PC Stewart."

The big man moved closer.

"I take it you have a warrant or such like to look at the records. Client confidentiality and all that."

DS Rose smiled.

"This is just a routine enquiry and I thought you might assist us with a few questions."

The man now smiled.

"Like I said, if you haven't got a warrant..."

Two more men now came out of the gym and stood beside 'Arnie'. They were equally as big.

"Do you know Tony Ellis, Chris Comer and Errol White?" asked DS Rose.

The man's face betrayed nothing.

"Well, I believe they used this gym," Rose continued, "They were all murdered last night."

The three men exchanged glances, but remained silent.

PC Stewart now walked forward. He was a big man himself, but these guys made him look small. Still, he carried authority to his voice when he spoke.

"We have reason to believe it could be somebody using this gym who committed the murders. That's why we're looking for help with our enquires."

'Arnie' regarded him.

"Why do you think it's a member of the gym?"

"Sorry," replied Stewart, "But we're not a liberty to disclose why."

"Well, in that case, I think we're done here. If you come back again, bring that warrant. I'll tell the boss when he gets back that you were here."

Stewart stared at the three men.

They returned his stare.

You could cut the tension in the air with a knife.

DS Rose intervened.

"Okay. Thank you. We'll be on our way for now."

"Yeah, you do that. Have a nice day," replied 'Arnie' sarcastically.

Outside, they walked back towards the car.

"Nice lads," said Stewart.

"Yeah, real charmers."

"Can we get a warrant to go back?" asked Stewart.

"I don't think we have enough evidence at this stage to warrant one if you excuse the pun. I'll have to ask the guv."

They both got back into the car.

As they pulled away, Kenny Stewart spoke.

"Those guys in that gym are fucking monsters, as were the three murdered. Our killer has got to be something special to go up against men like that."

Diane Rose nodded.

"Maybe he is the Terminator?"

Stewart laughed at the Arnold Schwarzenegger reference.

"Whoever he is, he must have specialist training. Maybe ex-military or a martial artist?"

"Whatever, he's one dangerous fucker," replied Rose.

Chapter 7

The four youths all sat on bikes in the small park across the road from the convenience store. They had their hoodies pulled up tight and scarves masking their faces.

Their plan was to rob the shop.

The leader of the gang was named Duane and his three oppos were Craig, Jacko and Finn. They had all been involved in a life of crime since they were knee high to a grasshopper. Duane's family were notorious in the area. Everybody tried to give them a wide berth if possible.

"Right, listen up," said Duane, "There's just the old man and his wife in the shop. Their two sons aren't about today, so this should be a piece of piss. We go in, flash our blades and shit them up, then do the cash register, ciggies, vapes and scratchcards. Then we're out of there. We hit them hard and fast. Understand?"

The other three nodded in unison.

"There's one CCTV camera in the shop. I'll take it out with this baseball bat."

Duane lifted his jacket to reveal it.

"Then, we'll have a free run of the place," he added.

* * *

The business was owned by an Asian family. The Patels.

The shop had been in this area of Bristol for over twenty-five years. It had been handed down in one shape or form in the family over time and was the legacy of all their hard work. It was well known locally and was always open every day from 7 to 11 for everything from a newspaper to a pint of milk.

Duane regarded the other youths.

"Finn, you stay outside and watch the door while we do the business. Let us know if the Old Bill come sniffing, although that's about as likely as me shagging Taylor Swift."

The boys all laughed.

Duane continued.

"Once we're done, we all cycle to the back of the old, deserted paintworks on Bridge St. We'll share out the cash there. My old man will have contacts that will take the rest of the stuff off our hands for a good price. As soon as he comes back from the match up at Sunderland tomorrow, he'll sort it, so don't fuck this up. I'm doing this little job off my own back. It's a rite of passage for us to move on to bigger things. We need to prove ourselves. I need to show my old man I'm capable and ready to play a bigger part in his empire."

Duane's father was Charlie Rawlings. At present, he was following his beloved 'Robins', Bristol City, as they took on Sunderland at the Stadium of Light on Tyneside.

In his younger days, Rawlings had been a notorious football thug, before progressing to becoming a minder for some shady characters. Working with these men led Charlie Rawlings into a business of money lending, extortion and drugs.

Rawlings' reputation proceeded him. You fucked with him and you got hurt.

One of the most notorious urban legends concerning the man was that he hunted down three men who owed him money. When they didn't pay, he took them all out with a machete, before dousing them in petrol and setting them alight.

Another claim to fame was that he went the distance back in the day in an unlicensed boxing match with the deceased legendary 'Guvnor' Lennie McLean in London.

Now in his early fifties, the man showed no signs of slowing down.

The police were well aware of Rawlings, but he had the nickname of 'Teflon Charlie' as nothing ever stuck on him.

In the South of Bristol, Charlie Rawlings was the 'guvnor.'

Charlie had lost his wife Cathy in childbirth. Duane was his only son and heir to his criminal empire.

The boy was 18 and, although not the sharpest tool in the box, he made up for this shortcoming with willingness and enthusiasm.

***

"We ready?" asked Duane.

"Yes," the others replied.

They all rode across the road and dropped their bikes outside the shop. The gang knew CCTV street cameras didn't cover this whole street, so they were more than confident that they could do this job.

Finn took his post at the door as the other three went inside. A bell tinged above the door as they entered. Once in the shop, the boys separated down different aisles.

They watched the counter and saw only Mrs Patel standing there. She was on the phone and briefly looked up to see who had entered the shop.

She registered the youths.

Wary because of constant shoplifting, the Patels had installed a CCTV monitor on the wall by the counter, which she now glanced at.

The local police had not been a great help in supporting them over the years. They were practically non-existent. Most didn't want to tangle with Charlie Rawlings. They opted instead for an easy life by burying their heads in the sand.

Unfortunately, the Patels had to learn to fend for themselves.

* * *

Mrs Patel couldn't see exactly how many youths there were as they had split off down different aisles of the shop.

She looked back at her phone once more as she finished off a text to her sister whose birthday it was today. Before she had a chance to press send, three youths ran up to the counter. The old woman dropped the phone in shock.

"Right, do exactly as I tell you and you won't get hurt!"

Duane brandished the bat and swung it at the CCTV monitor, smashing it.

He regarded the old woman.

"I want you to open the till," he said.

The woman stood frozen to the spot in fear.

"Do you fucking hear me? Open the till now!"

The three youths now all drew knives.

Duane grabbed a plastic carrier bag and threw it to Mrs Patel.

"Put the money in there."

Mrs Patel slowly moved to the till and opened it. Her hands shook as she took out the money and put it into the bag.

"Hurry. Faster!" said Duane.

Jacko looked over towards him.

"We'll take the ciggies, vapes and scratchcards."

Duane looked behind the counter to the stocked shelves.

"Yeah, alright. This old bird is taking too fucking long here. Take a bag and fill it."

Jacko ran around the counter, just as Mr Patel came in from the back room carrying two mugs of tea.

"Here we go. I didn't know if you wanted a biscuit. I can open…"

His words froze in his mouth as he saw the three youths.

"What the hell are you doing?" he asked.

Jacko pushed him out of the way. The elderly man staggered back into the shelving behind him and the mugs of tea crashed to the floor.

"Stay still, granddad and don't fucking move," hissed Jacko.

"Please don't hurt us," pleaded Mrs Patel, "My husband is not a well man. He has a heart condition."

"Shut the fuck up and hand us that money. That better be all of it." snarled Duane.

He now regarded Craig.

"Right, get behind that counter and help out."

Craig moved behind the counter. As he did so, Mr Patel grabbed at the youth's coat latching on to it.

"No, you don't. I will not have you stealing from us, you scum. This is our livelihood. We work hard for what we have. You can't just come in and take it."

Craig spun around to break Mr Patel's grip on his jacket and instinctively thrust out with the knife he had in his hand. The blade sank into the old man's belly.

Mr Patel staggered back, looking at the blood stain spreading on his shirt front.

Mrs Patel screamed.

Jacko grabbed her and clamped a hand over her mouth.

"Let's get the fuck out of here!" shouted Jacko.

"Not until we get all we came for," replied Duane.

He looked down at the old man.

"You really should have done what you were told, you old fool."

* * *

The black transit van pulled up across the road from the Patels.

Michael's stomach was rumbling as he got out. He couldn't recall the last time he had eaten a meal. He would quickly nip into the store, get his shopping and then head over to the café for some breakfast. He felt a couple of 'doorstep' bacon sarnies and a mug of tea coming on. First came some groceries, though.

As he walked towards the shop, he saw a youth furtively lurking by the door puffing on a vape. He instantly sensed something wasn't right. When he drew level, the youth regarded him.

"Shop's shut, mate. Some sort of power cut or something."

Michael looked through the window.

"Looks like there are lights on in there to me."

He went to try the door and that's when the youth called Finn pulled a knife.

"Just fuck off back in your van, pal, and forget you were here."

Michael impassively regarded the knife.

"Now that's not very friendly. I suggest you see sense and put that away now."

"Listen, mister. Don't think I'm bluffing. I will fucking stick you."

"Is that so? Well, in that case, you better make your move because I'm starving and in a bad mood."

Before Finn could back up his threat, Michael moved fast and slapped the knife hand away from the line of his body, sending the knife flying, before launching a crunching kick with his boot into Finn's balls.

The youth dropped to his knees like a stone. The follow-up kick to his jaw put him to sleep.

Michael opened the shop door and walked in.

The bell alerted the three youths inside. Loaded with their contraband, they were ready to leave.

Michael quickly assessed the situation.

"Well, well, well, what have we here then?"

Duane brandished his bat.

"Get the fuck out of the way, man, or you'll get hurt."

Michael smiled.

"Funny, your unconscious buddy outside told me the same thing a few moments ago."

Duane screwed his face up with hate.

"Fuck you, asshole. You had your warning."

He ran forward, ready to swing the bat.

Michael moved inside the arc of the bat and jammed it. He headbutted Duane solidly in the face, making him release his weapon. As the youth staggered backwards, his face a mask of blood, Michael thrust the end of the bat into Duane's stomach, sending him to the floor.

Then, Michael swung the bat into Jacko's right knee, shattering it instantly. The screaming lad hit the floor and the big man stomped on his head.

Michael now fronted Craig, who lunged at him with his blade. He brought the bat down on the youth's knife wrist, breaking his radius bone like a stick of celery and then swung it into the back of his head. He too went down.

Wiping blood from his face, Duane pulled himself back to standing and pulled his knife.

"You are fucking dead. Do you know what family I belong to?"

Michael stared at the lad impassively.

"Why don't you enlighten me, you piece of shit? Is it the Simpsons by any chance?"

"The fucking Rawlings family. We own this area. My old man is Charlie Rawlings. He'll cut your fucking balls off for this."

Somewhere in the distance, Michael heard a police siren.

He had to go.

"Well, that's good to know, kid. Now, put that bag down and fuck off, before you join your mates. You're lucky that I'm sparing you your life."

Duane looked at his fallen comrades, then at the big man in front of him holding his baseball bat. This guy didn't look intimidated in any shape or form.

He also heard the sirens. He knew his best option was to flee.

Duane dropped the bag and edged towards the door, never taking his eyes off the man. As he opened the door, he looked back.

"My family will find you and do you in for this, I promise. You're fucking dead."

"Maybe I'll find them first. Now fuck off!"

Duane left the shop, got on his bike and pedalled away quickly.

The man now looked towards the old lady stood at the counter.

"Did you ring the police?" he asked her.

"Yes, and the ambulance. They stabbed my husband."

Michael dropped the bat, moved forward and went behind the counter. He regarded the man sat on the floor. Mr Patel was pressing a towel to his stomach. His skin pallor was ashen.

Michael crouched down, eased the towel away carefully and studied the wound. He had seen many different types of wounds before in the past. This one looked worse than it was.

"Just keep pressing the cloth tight. You'll be okay. Help is on its way."

The old man nodded and smiled weakly.

Mrs Patel now spoke.

"Thank you so much for your help."

"No need to thank me. I guess I was in the right place at the right time."

The sirens were now close.

He regarded Mrs Patel.

"Is there a back way out of here?"

"Yes."

"I have to go."

"Go through that door and on into the kitchen. Go out the back door."

Michael nodded.

"Wait. You saved us from robbery and I don't even know your name."

The big man stopped and looked over his shoulder.

"Call me Michael."

As two police cars skidded to a halt outside the front of the shop, Michael disappeared out the back.

* * *

An hour later, the police had rounded up the three unconscious youths. They were all admitted under escort to the hospital.

Mr Patel was also brought to hospital and was comfortable for now. The knife wound was not serious, fortunately.

The police got the full details of what had happened from Mrs Patel. A Sergeant Jack Hart from the local nick interviewed her.

When it came to who the man was who had intervened and foiled the robbery, Mrs Patel could only recall that he was tall, well built and dressed in all black. He had said that his name was Michael. He had apparently left the scene without saying anything else.

She did tell them that there had been another youth in the shop who appeared to be the leader. For some reason, the man had let him go.

When the three youths recovered enough to talk, they reinforced what Mrs Patel had said. The man had been big and dressed head to toe in black and had been a vicious bastard.

It had all happened so fast that they couldn't remember anything else. They did state, however, that there hadn't been a fourth person helping them and that the old lady had made a mistake.

The police suspected that was a lie and they were protecting whoever it was. The police also knew that these lads hung out with Duane Rawlings and this had his stamp all over it, although they had no actual proof he had been there.

A baseball bat had been recovered from the scene and it was taken away for forensic analysis.

The three youths were out of hospital and in custody Monday morning.

For now, Duane Rawlings remained free.

As for this Michael character, he had seemed to have vanished into thin air.

Sergeant Jack Hart couldn't make up his mind if this man called Michael was a villain or a hero. He presumed most people in this area would see him as the latter as Rawlings and his brood were hated. Still, it bothered him that this man hadn't stayed around to give his side of the story.

Maybe he was just a Good Samaritan chancing by who didn't want any involvement or publicity. The beating he had administered out, though, bothered Hart for some reason.

These kids were street smart and tough. Plus, they had all been armed. But that hadn't seemed to bother the mystery man.

Chapter 8

Trent Lewis drove his van towards his final job of Monday afternoon. He was on the way to do the last of six boiler services. He had his own heating and plumbing business and as you would expect at this time of the year, he was busy.

As he drove, he thought of the past weekend just gone. The big bust-up with Dawn was at the forefront of his mind.

He well and truly believed this time it was over between them.

He hadn't called or texted her since early Sunday when he had last seen her outside the club. He had also heard nothing from her either.

Trent had been so angry with her that he had just blurted out the first hurtful things that had come into his head. Mind you, Dawn had given as good as she got.

It was a mess. He wasn't sure what to do and his throbbing headache didn't help.

Last night, he met his best mate Gaz down the local pub to unburden himself of his problems. After too many pints and a few whisky chasers, the situation was still no clearer.

* * *

Trent spotted a newsagent shop and decided to pull in to get himself a can of Red Bull to see if it would liven him up a little to finish off the job. He entered the shop, headed for the fridge and retrieved a can.

As he waited in a small queue to pay, his eye caught the newspaper stand and particularly the front page of the lunchtime copy of *The Bristol Eye*.

He saw a photograph of something that looked very familiar.

A bracelet. Exactly like the one he had bought Dawn for her birthday a few months back. In fact, it was identical.

Grabbing a copy of the paper, he paid for his purchases and headed back to his van.

Once inside, he scanned the headlines and was horrified to learn that this bracelet had been found at a brutal murder scene. His blood ran cold when further down the article he read that the bracelet had an inscription that read *To Dawn, Love Trent*.

Trent was momentarily in shock.

Jesus Christ, this is Dawn's bracelet. How in the hell did it get to be at a murder scene?

Fear now gripped him.

He pulled out his mobile phone and rang Dawn's number. After a dozen rings, it went to voicemail.

He looked at the time. It was 4:15pm. She was probably still in work. He hoped to God she was.

The three dead men were supposedly the killers of the young girl in Bristol city centre a few months back. The police suggested Dawn might have been another intended victim, but seemed to have got away.

Trent hoped that was the case.

The article said that the bracelet was found in the back of the men's van. Opinion was that the girl had fled the scene and told nobody what had occurred.

The police pleaded with her to come forward.

Dawn worked at Cut and Curl Hair Salon. It was about a ten-minute drive away.

Trent decided to head there. On the way, he tried her number again, but without success.

* * *

Trent pulled up outside the salon, jumped out his van and headed for the door.

On opening it, he saw Valerie Fields, the salon owner, at the reception.

Valerie was a good-looking woman in her fifties with eye-catching platinum blonde hair piled high on top of her head in a beehive.

He hurried over to her.

Valerie saw him coming.

"If you're here to see Dawn, don't bother. She doesn't want to see you."

Trent ignored the jibe.

"Is Dawn here? Is she okay?"

Valerie eyed the young man and sensed fear in his voice.

She immediately softened her stance.

"What's wrong Trent?"

"I haven't got time to explain. Is she here and is she okay?"

"Yes, she's in the back and as far as I know, she's fine, apart from being pissed off with you."

Trent felt his patience fraying.

"Shut the fuck up, Valerie. I need to see her now."

The older woman looked shocked.

"Now wait a minute…"

Trent suddenly saw Dawn appear from the back room and he ran over to her.

Dawn saw him coming and held up her hands.

"I don't want to see you, Trent. Please leave me alone."

Trent slowed down his pace.

"Have you seen the paper this morning?"

Dawn was thrown out by the question.

"What?"

Trent pulled the copy of *The Bristol Eye* from his coat pocket and handed it to her.

Dawn scanned the front page and her face drained of blood. It looked for all the world like she was going to faint. Trent reached out and grabbed her in his arms.

"You were there, weren't you? You have to go to the police. What happened, Dawn? Please tell me."

Dawn caught her breath and composure.

"I didn't know what to do. It seemed all so unreal and I was so drunk."

"You need to tell me everything now," said Trent.

Dawn nodded.

"Okay. But not here."

Valerie walked over.

"Is everything alright, Dawn? I told him to leave…"

"It's fine, Valerie. I'm going to talk to Trent, but I need some privacy if that's okay. Can you manage without me for 15 minutes if I pop over the road to Sheila's Café?"

Valerie's eyes moved from Dawn to Trent and then back again.

"Yes. If that's what you want. I'm here if you need me."

Dawn squeezed the older woman's arm.

"Thank you, Val. I'll make up the time in my lunch tomorrow."

With that, they both left the salon and headed across the road to the café.

* * *

At a corner table with two coffees in front of them, Dawn related the horrific story of early Sunday morning. Trent couldn't believe his ears. He held Dawn's hand tightly as she told it.

It was like something out of a horror movie.

When she finished, Trent shook his head in disbelief.

"And you were just going to say nothing and carry on as normal?"

Dawn nodded.

"This stranger saved my life. I knew at one point these men were going to rape and kill me, just like that young girl. I would be dead now if not for him. I don't care what he did to those evil bastards. They can't hurt anybody ever again. I didn't want to get this man in trouble. I thought if I ignored things and carried on as normal, it would all go away."

Trent leaned closer to her.

"I understand that and I'm truly grateful you came to no harm, but this dude wasted three men and walked off. People can't just do that. They've got to be answerable for their actions."

"Like you and those little tarts the other night?" asked Dawn.

Trent swallowed hard.

"Yes. Just like that. But let's talk about that later."

Tears welled up in Dawn's eyes.

"This man saved me."

Trent tried to keep control of his emotions.

"Dawn, think rationally. This guy coming across the scene and giving these men a bit of a kick-in is one thing and probably acceptable, but going through them all with a big fucking knife is something different altogether. This man can't be right in the head, which makes him unpredictable. Maybe he'll decide to come back and find you, seeing you're the only witness. You've got to tell the police what you know for your own safety. Who knows what this guy is capable of? But all I know is he's here in Bristol walking the streets and he's a killer. We don't know what he'll do next."

"But he didn't harm me. He just told me to go home."

"Listen, Dawn baby. A man who just comes out of nowhere and cuts three men up for sausage meat and doesn't flinch is fucking dangerous and needs to be caught. We're going to the police now and telling them everything. If you don't come, I'm going there and telling them that the bracelet is yours."

Dawn sighed and hung her head.

"Why are you here, Trent?"

"What do you mean?"

"We said all we had to say to each other on Sunday. We are through."

Trent gently pulled Dawn's face up and looked into her eyes.

"I'm here because I love you and I care for you. Yes, I know I can be a prick and if you don't want to see me again when we've done this, then I understand, but when I read the newspaper, I was scared for you and I was afraid you were hurt or worse. I couldn't have lived with myself. You've got to believe me. You were walking home on your own because of my selfish actions. The whole terrible incident could have been avoided if I hadn't been a dick."

Dawn began to gently weep.

Trent stroked her face.

"Please, baby. Let's go to the police and tell them everything. You'll be okay, I promise."

Dawn looked at Trent.

"And then what?"

Trent smiled sadly.

"Let's cross that bridge when we come to it."

* * *

DCI Harry Bowe sat at his desk sipping a coffee, which was slightly better than the one he had out of the machine yesterday. The three sugars may have had something to do with it.

He was deep in thought when a knock on his office door brought him out of his reverie.

He looked up to see DS Rose standing there.

"Got a minute, sir?"

"Yes, of course. Come in, Diane. What is it?"

"I think we might have a break in the case."

"In that case, take a seat and tell me more."

Harry gestured to the small leather sofa.

DS. Rose sat down.

"I've just had an interesting conversation with a young lady named Dawn Little, the owner of the bracelet."

"You're fucking kidding me!" exclaimed Harry.

"No, sir. She came in with her boyfriend and gave us a statement."

"What did she say?" asked Harry.

DS Rose went on to disclose her full story. When finished, Harry softly whistled.

"So, she witnessed the lot. She was targeted as a victim, but ended up surviving and seeing the man who committed the murders."

"That's about the sum of it. The description isn't great. He was dressed head to toe in black. She never really saw his features clearly. He had a beanie hat on and he was sporting many days of beard growth. She thinks he was 6' plus and solidly built. Here's the thing. When she asked him who he was, he replied Michael. Earlier she had heard him tell the men that he was here to do his duty or something like that."

Harry chewed on the end of his pencil as he listened.

"Accent?" he asked.

Rose consulted her notebook.

"Nothing distinctive."

Harry nodded.

"Okay. It's something to go on. At least we now know this man exists and he's human."

Rose smiled.

"Not a ghost after all then."

Harry smiled back.

"Apparently not. Good work, Diane. Get that description and name circulating around. Get a forensic artist sketching up an image for the media. We have her address if we need to follow up?" he asked.

Rose nodded.

"Yes, sir."

"Get hold of Jim and give him the description of this Michael. Tell him when he's looking through the CCTV footage outside the Jungle Club to keep an eye out for this man."

"I'll get straight on it. Dawn also mentioned she had started her evening in the Pacifica nightclub on Greyfriars Street. I think it's worth checking their CCTV as well, sir."

"Good call. You deal with that yourself," replied Bowe.

"I wonder what he meant by doing his duty?" pondered Harry.

Rose stood up.

"I don't know, sir. Oh, by the way, I didn't have any luck at the Vault Gym. The owner wasn't there, and the staff weren't too cooperative. We'll need a warrant if we want to see their records."

"Okay, Diane. We'll hang fire with that for the moment and see if this latest lead takes us anywhere."

* * *

When DS Rose had left the room, he picked up the phone and called Tommy Good.

Good picked up on the second ring.

"Goodie, it's DCI Bowe. We've just had a small break on the case. Here's an update for you."

Harry brought him up to speed.

"Listen, Goodie," he added, "You know I've always given you first shout on a story. Well, the big boy tabloids are on my case and pushing hard, so is the television. This new information about the killer calling himself Michael and the sketch I'll send over as soon as possible are only available to you today, before I have to speak to the press and media tomorrow afternoon."

Goodie nodded.

"Much appreciated, Harry. I'll run this story first thing in the morning and get a head start on them. I'll also get a few sources of mine out on the streets armed with this new intel. Get them to shake a few trees and see who or what drops out."

"Okay, Goodie. If this is the name the killer goes by, somebody somewhere must know him or have a suspicion. He's got to go home somewhere," replied the DCI.

"Harry, can I ask why you think he's started killing now here in Bristol?"

"I have a few theories in my head, but they're only theories. So, off the record, either he has been planning and working his way up to doing this for some time or he's moved to Bristol from another part of the country. I'll get some of my team asking other police departments across the UK if there have been any similar murders or if the name Michael has cropped up. It's a lot of work, but I tend to lean towards the theory that this man has killed before and has moved to Bristol recently. The manner of the killings doesn't suggest a novice. There are another few lines of inquiry I can also pursue, but they can wait for now."

"Okay, Harry. You'll keep me up to speed, won't you?" said Goodie.

Harry got up from his chair.

"Of course. The same goes for you if you turn up anything. We have to nail this bastard before he strikes again. There's no way we can protect every criminal in this city. It's a rich hunting ground for this lunatic.

The killings are random in nature. As far as I know, the victims didn't know each other or are connected in any other way bar the fact that they were all known criminals."

"This guy must have his ear on the streets to know about these types of people. You aren't going to find them on Facebook or Instagram," replied Goodie.

Harry laughed.

"What a pity. It would make my job a lot easier."

He headed to the door.

"I'll keep in touch."

Chapter 9

Camp Bastion, Northwest of the city of Lashkargah in Helmand Province, 2015

Captain Mick Lange was walking down a long dark corridor towards a shining light. As he got closer to the light, he could hear voices, although they were indistinguishable at that point.

His life was flashing in front of his eyes as if somebody was flicking through a picture book. He saw himself as a child, his school days, then becoming a man, then a soldier. His life was documented before him from the cradle and now presumably to the grave. A feeling of serenity washed over Lange and also an acceptance that this was how it was going to be.

As he got ever closer to the light, he felt a warmness flood through his body and then a gentle voice spoke clearly to him.

"My son, you have been brought here before your time. I am sending you home. The world needs a man like you. You still have a job to do, but no longer in the British military. You will still be a soldier, but you will be a soldier of God.

You Michael 'Mick' Lange will become my dispenser of justice on earth. You will become Michael the Archangel. His human self.

He is the spiritual warrior in the battle of good versus evil. He is the champion of justice, a guardian of the church. He escorts people into the afterlife. He has the power to decide whether a soul goes to heaven or hell.

You, Michael, will become my conduit to the evils of the earth and you will do all you can to eradicate the influence of Satan and restore the balance of nature, before this earth I created will be destroyed by the very people in it.

There are others like you scattered across the four corners of the earth, all battling evil for salvation. All doing my bidding.

Time to go back, Michael Lange. Go back and begin your new vocation in life.

Remember, I am with you just like I was with you in the desert when you were lost and dying and you asked for my help.

But with any help, there is always a price to be paid.

You will now become my soul catcher.

God bless you, my son, and good hunting."

The voice disappeared and Captain Mick Lange started going backwards. Everything he could see was going in reverse.

He now heard the voice of his father.

"Michael, at last you have accepted God, as I hoped you would someday. Do as he says, and your soul will be spared from redemption. I love you and someday we will reunite. Your mother sends her love."

Then, the voice faded.

As he passed different points in his life, those memories were erased from his mind.

He now caught a glimpse of young Joe Eccles waving and smiling at him. Then, he faded away.

When he eventually had awoken, he was no longer Captain Mick Lange of the Special Air Service. He was Michael the Archangel.

He now had a new mission and a new agenda.

The people would rejoice when they heard his name.

They would pray.

Defend us in battle. Be our protection against the wickedness and snares of the Devil.

Michael was now only answerable to God himself.

* * *

Captain Mick Lange awoke to find himself in a hospital bed. He had little memory of how he had got here. He did recall walking off into the night after the disastrous and tragic mission, wounded and lost.

Visions of his slaughtered comrades came into his mind. He inwardly shuddered.

Somehow, he had walked out of that barren desert land and into a British patrol base, where he had collapsed unconscious on the floor.

The patrol base was for British soldiers to watch and monitor situations in the surrounding area. It was only about eight by eight metres, but it provided a safe haven out in the desert.

Somehow, through impossible odds, Lange had found it and was still clinging onto life.

Each base had a sangar or watchtower. A soldier on guard duty had picked up the lone figure of Lange practically crawling to the base. After basic first aid treatment, Lange had been flown by helicopter to Camp Bastion.

Camp Bastion was then the main British base in Afghanistan and the main specialist medical hub for the British Armed Forces. Built by the British army in 2005-06, it could accommodate up to two thousand people. It was four miles long and ten miles wide. Not only did it house the hospital, but it also contained a busy airfield.

The hospital was a busy place for soldiers wounded by explosive devices or bullets. By the end of the conflict, there would be 453 deaths of British soldiers.

As the days went by, Lange learnt that he had undergone an operation to have two bullets removed from his torso. Both miraculously did not hit any internal organs.

On arrival, he had lost a serious amount of blood, and it was touch and go for a while on the operating table. At one point, the surgeon had lost him. For two minutes, he had been clinically dead. But Lange fought back and he was finally stabilised.

In the end, the operation had been a success.

Both his eardrums had been perforated and it would take up to six to eight weeks for them to heal and for his hearing to return properly. He also had a piece of shrapnel stuck in his left calf. Again, he was fortunate; it had only damaged muscle and tendon, but the injury would leave him with a slight limp.

It really was a miracle that he was alive.

To complete his recovery, Lange had been flown to the Royal Centre for Defence Medicine in Birmingham, England. His tour of Afghanistan was well and truly over.

Although he gradually recovered from his physical injuries, the mental trauma left with Lange from his time in Afghanistan was significant. He seemed confused and lost one minute and then he would be angry and aggressive in the next. He told army psychiatrists that he had seen God and he had spoken with him. He told them that God had spared his life to do his work on earth. He was now waiting for a sign to begin.

He refused now to be called Mick and wanted to be referred to as Michael.

So, after exhaustive tests and analyses, Captain Michael 'Mick' Lange was discharged on PTSD grounds from the Armed Forces and was given follow-up psychiatric care. He had many ghosts to lay to rest.

He was also told that he and his team were in an ongoing government investigation accusing them of war crimes, but he was lucky as his psychological state of mind would make him exempt from giving evidence. He was told to make an immediate appointment to carry on his care.

Lange had other plans though.

He got lost in the system and went off the grid. Lange became a forgotten man, which suited him fine. He had work to do.

But first, he had to get fit again and prepare himself physically and mental for the task ahead.

Chapter 10

Sergeant Jack Hart regarded the front page of *The Bristol Eye*. He began to read the latest developments in the case of the so-called 'Ghost' killings. He was sat behind his desk at Westbury Road Police Station.

He stopped at the point where it read that a young woman had gone into the main police headquarters in the centre of Bristol and told police officers in charge of the case that she had seen 'The Ghost' and he had told her that his name was Michael.

Something rang a bell inside Jack Hart's head, and he looked around on his cluttered desk for his notebook. Once he located it, he turned the pages until he found his notes on the incident in the Patels' shop the other day.

There it was. The thing that had niggled him.

Mr and Mrs Patel had both said that the man who had saved them from robbery and had sorted out their would-be attackers told them that his name was Michael.

Jesus. Could this be the same guy?

He checked Dawn Little's description of the man and ran it against the Patels.

It was almost identical.

The way the man had dispatched the youths had made Hart uneasy. Now he realised why.

He immediately reached for his phone and dialled the number of Central HQ. Once connected, he asked to speak to DCI Harry Bowe.

* * *

Harry was halfway through his lunch of a BLT sandwich and an orange juice as his desk phone buzzed.

He picked it up.

The desk sergeant told him that DS Jack Hart was on the line.

Harry took the call.

Jack Hart was an old colleague of his and a good friend. It had been a while since they had spoken.

"How you doing, Jack, you old bastard?" asked Harry.

Jack laughed.

"Not as well as you, Harry, I suspect."

"It's been a while, my old friend. What can I do for you?"

"Well, it's more of what I think I can do for you."

Harry put his sandwich down on the desk.

"Okay, now you've got me intrigued. What is it?"

Over the next ten minutes, Jack Hart told Harry about the incident at the Patels and the man called Michael. As Harry digested the information, he felt a tingle of adrenaline in the pit of his stomach.

"Is there any CCTV in the shop?" asked Harry.

"There was a monitor by the counter, but one of the youths smashed it with a baseball bat."

"Shit!" exclaimed the frustrated DCI, "What about outside the shop? Any cameras nearby?"

"There are cameras, but they're not fixed on that particular area of the street."

"They bloody wouldn't be, would they? This guy leads a charmed fucking life."

"Harry, I'm going to run through CCTV footage in the area around that time. Maybe I can turn up something. I'm presuming this guy drove to the shop. It might be worth a shout checking out any vehicles on the road at that time."

"Okay, Jack. Keep me up to speed if you find anything."

"Righto, Harry. We also believe that Duane Rawlings is the missing fourth member of the attempted raid. Somehow, he got away. He seems to have gone to ground at present. I think he would have had a good look at this man and can give us a good description."

"I'll get on this and see if we can track him down," said Harry, "Any known haunts he might be hiding out at?"

"Could be anywhere, Harry. Max's Snooker Hall, Golden Nugget arcade, the Vault Gym…"

Harry interrupted him.

"The Vault Gym. He goes there, does he?"

"Yeah. His old man Charlie and a lot of his cronies work out there. If the devil casted his net, he would make a right catch."

Harry took the information on board and then finished the call. He sat back in his chair, chewing over this latest news.

The three dead men were from the Vault Gym. The Rawlings' family used it. The place was getting more interesting by the minute. Harry had a small voice in his head telling him that the gym held a clue to who this mystery man was.

He needed to pay it a visit himself.

Chapter 11

"What the fuck do you mean some bloke just walked in the shop and slapped you all around like bitches? Who was this joker? What did he look like?"

"I don't know, Dad. I've never seen him before. He was a big dude. Dressed in black. He wore a beanie hat pulled down tight on his head. He had a beard."

Charlie Rawlings and his son Duane were sat in the saloon bar of the White Hart pub.

Charlie had arrived home a little earlier today in a good mood. Bristol City had beat Sunderland 2-1 and he had been celebrating all weekend up in Tyneside before driving back home.

He was nursing the daddy of all headaches and had been looking forward to crashing out in bed. His good mood had been dampened somewhat by Duane ringing him and delivering the news.

Charlie was not impressed that his son had decided to take on a job without his say so. Not only that, but he had fucked it up royally and had the police on his tail. He had also not expected the news from Duane about some stranger riding to the rescue of the Patels and beating the shit out of his son and his crew.

"He gave no name or message?" asked Charlie.

"No, Dad. He said nothing. He just told me he would spare me and let me go."

Duane squirmed embarrassingly under his father's gaze.

"Cheeky bastard. So, this isn't some geezer on some sort of revenge mission against me or the family?"

"I don't think so. I think he just randomly walked in on us. When I told him who I was and the family name, he didn't show a flicker of concern or recognition."

Charlie Rawlings chewed this information over.

"Well, he will know the name Rawlings by the time I've finished with him. You know this bastard can't get away with this, don't you? If word gets out that you had your ass handed to you and your boys were burnt like toast, every chancer will try to take a pop at us, and I can't let that happen. I need retribution in the way of bloodshed."

Duane nodded sullenly.

"You've been a complete twat here, my son. I don't know what you were thinking, especially taking those muppet friends of yours along. Robbing a place practically on your doorstep is one thing, but stabbing the old man is fucking crazy. If the police can prove you were there, you'll do time, you know that," said Charlie, "Any knife crime these days can be a ten stretch."

"I was only trying to do something to prove myself," replied Duane.

"You did that alright, boy. You proved you're a fucking loser. To stay in this game, you have to have brain first and brawn second. How do you think I've stayed out of prison for so long? You know that's what I've always taught you. You know the coppers will be around to our gaff sticking their fucking oar in my business and I can't afford that happening, especially not now. In the meanwhile, you better keep a low profile until I can sort this out. Understand? And make sure your mates keep their mouths shout!"

"Yes, Dad."

"I also want to find this joker who beat on you."

"He might have just been passing through and not in Bristol anymore, Dad," said Duane.

Charlie regarded his son.

"That might be the case, but we won't know until we've made sure that this geezer isn't here for something else. You know I got a big drug deal coming up soon with the Albanian crew. There's big bucks to be made if they decide to let me in on the deal. They're tough people to negotiate with and dangerous fuckers. I want to make sure the playing field is clear and that nobody else is trying to muscle in."

"Like I said, Dad, he just seemed an ordinary geezer," replied Duane.

"Ordinary. Fucking ordinary. There were four of you armed with knives and he went through you without breaking sweat. Whoever this person is, he ain't fucking ordinary, my son. When he went in that shop, he could have run back out again, but he chose not to, and I want to know why. Now, get your ass out of here and keep your ear to the ground. Bring me back some good news."

"What if the police come asking questions?" said Duane.

"I'll handle that. Now go! Stay at your Uncle Dennis's house and keep out of trouble. If the police do find you, say nothing until I get to you. Understand? Put your uncle in the picture too."

Duane slung on his jacket and slumped out the pub with his tail firmly between his legs.

When he had gone, Charlie headed to the bar and ordered another whisky. There was too much at stake just to dismiss this incident without looking into it further.

As he walked back to his chair, he picked up a newspaper lying on a tabletop nearby. It was a copy of *The Bristol Eye*.

He glanced at the headlines.

His blood suddenly ran cold.

He read the story about the three murdered doormen. Charlie knew them all well. From the Jungle Club and also the gym. They had done a bit of business together in the past when he needed a bit of extra muscle for debt collecting or drug selling. They were solid boys to call on. Whoever took them all out must be right tasty.

As he read on, his heartrate quickened when he saw the description of the would-be killer.

Tall, dressed head to toe in black, wearing a beanie hat. His name is Michael.

He didn't believe in coincidences. This sounded like the same man who had attacked Duane and his crew in the convenience store.

Charlie Rawlings now pressed speed dial on his phone. He called Ed Lyons, the owner of the Vault Gym.

Ed answered almost instantly.

"Guess you saw the paper, Charlie?"

"Yeah, I saw it. I'm on my way over to the gym for a chat. Be available."

"Sure thing. I'll be here," replied Joe.

* * *

Charlie Rawlings pulled his BMW up outside the Vault Gym. He jumped out the car and entered the building.

Ed Lyons was sat at the reception. He was in his mid-sixties with greying hair and a sunbed tan. He was still in good shape for a man of advancing age.

He looked up as Charlie entered.

He mused that Rawlings always carried that air of menace in his 100kg frame, shaven head and a myriad of tattoos.

"Alright, Charlie. Let's talk in my office."

Both men made their way through reception and through a door marked private into a small and cluttered office. Ed cleared some paperwork off a battered leather seat and gestured to Charlie.

"Sit down. Drink?"

Charlie nodded.

Ed opened a filing cabinet and fished out a half empty bottle of Jura malt and two glasses. He put them down on his desk and poured two generous measures, handing one to Charlie. He then took a seat behind his desk.

Charlie took a swig of whisky. It tasted good. He then looked across at the other man.

"What the fuck happened to Ellis, Comer and White?"

Ed sipped his own drink.

"You know as much as me. I came back last night, and our Zoe told me that the coppers had been around wanting to look at the member records and saying that they thought somebody here in the gym knew something about the murders."

"What do you think, Ed?" asked Rawlings.

"Everybody here is shocked. They all respected and liked the boys. I've heard nothing otherwise in here. Besides, I know we get some tough guys in this gym, but to take on Tony Ellis and the other boys, they would have to be fucking mad. I still can't believe one man just carved them up."

Rawlings nodded.

"Any idea who this fucking lunatic might be that killed them?"

Ed topped up his drink.

"Not a fucking clue, Charlie. Whoever he is has got a pair, I give him that."

"Not somebody muscling in from the other side of Bristol?"

Ed shook his head.

"No chance, Charlie. Johnny Riggs and his crew know to stay their side of the water. They aren't going to rock the boat. Everybody knows this is your patch. Nobody is going to fuck with you, are they?"

Charlie swallowed his drink down.

"You'd like to think so, but I'm not so sure."

Charlie went on to tell Joe about what had happened to Duane and his mates, but swore Ed to secrecy.

"And you think this is the same geezer who did the killings?" said Ed.

"Yes. I believe it is. And if it is, I need to find him and put him away. You know the Albanians are on their way. I can't afford any fuck-ups."

"Okay, Charlie. I'll pass the word around the gym to the boys and see what they can find out. If he is out there, we'll track him down."

Charlie got up to leave and then sat back down again.

"Are you sure nobody strange has joined the gym? Anybody feel out of place?"

Ed shook his head.

"No, Charlie. Coming up to Christmas, you don't get any new members signing up. That normally happens in the new year. It's been quiet."

This time, Charlie did stand up and went to the door.

"As I said, keep me up to speed if you hear anything."

* * *

When Charlie left the office, he thought that he would walk into the gym to see who was about. As he entered, he almost tripped over a metal bucket of soapy water. He sidestepped it and saw a cleaner in blue overalls mopping down the cardio machines.

Charlie shouted over to him.

"Hey! You wanna be careful where you leave that fucking bucket, pal."

The man was engrossed in his work and had earbuds in. He never looked up.

Charlie was about to head over to him when a man over in the weight section shouted out in his direction.

"Hey, Charlie. You got a moment to spot me on this bench press?"

Charlie Rawlings glanced over and saw it was his old buddy and one of his top boys in the firm, Gerry Tucker.

"Yeah, sure thing, Gerry."

As he headed towards his friend, he took one more backward glance at the man cleaning. He was still intensely mopping the treadmills and never looked up or acknowledged him.

* * *

Michael looked up from his cleaning and watched the man walk over to the weights area.

He flicked out his earbuds. They weren't connected to anything. This was how he could walk around the gym and eavesdrop on conversations without anybody knowing.

He had visited the gym not long after coming to Bristol and asked the owner Ed Lyons if he had any work going. Michael had been in luck as Lyons' cleaner had left the previous week.

The job was a few hours each day. Cash in hand. No questions asked. Nothing on the books.

Michael took it.

The job had led him to overhearing Ellis, Comer and White talking about targeting another girl on Saturday. His tipoff had been correct again.

The job had just been handed to Michael on a plate. The Lord does move in mysterious ways. He had been glad of the guidance.

* * *

Duane Rawlings was in Max's Snooker Hall playing the final frame of his match when the cops walked in. He had gone to his Uncle Dennis's and his girlfriend had told him that he was down at the snooker club, so Duane went looking for him.

Three Jack Daniels and Coke and a joint later, he was feeling more relaxed and mellow. Uncle Dennis was out on a bit of business, but coming back to the club later.

Duane decided to play a few frames whilst he waited.

On seeing Harry Bowe, he dropped the cue and ran towards the back entrance just as DS Ali Khan came through it. Duane turned back the other way to encounter DCI Harry Bowe's imposing frame.

Harry regarded the youth's battered face.

"Looks like you've been in a war already, my son. I don't think you want another, do you? So, don't do anything silly."

Duane slumped against the wall.

"We'd like a little chat with you down at the station," continued Harry.

"Am I under arrest or what?" asked Duane.

Harry regarded the youth.

"At the minute, we're at the 'or what' stage, but if you co-operate with us, it may be to your benefit."

"What do you want to talk about?"

"The robbery at Patel's on Sunday that you organised," said Harry.

"Don't know what you're talking about," retorted Duane.

"Well, we have evidence to the contrary."

"I don't fucking believe you, man."

"We have CCTV of you and your buddies lurking outside the shop," replied DS Khan.

"Is that right?" sneered Duane, "You can make a positive ID, can you? See my face, did you?"

Harry ignored the question, knowing full well that Rawlings had been hooded and scarfed up and the little prick knew it also.

"We also have a baseball bat found at the scene of the crime with your prints all over it, so you're banged to rights."

Duane Rawlings started laughing.

"You fucking muppets. That's a lie. I was wearing gloves…"

Suddenly, the youth knew that he had been drawn into a trap.

"Never the sharpest tool in the box were you, Duane?" said Harry.

Suddenly, the youth's bravado had disappeared like bath water down the plug hole.

"I want to call my dad."

"You can get one phone call at the station if need be. DS Khan, read him his rights, will you?"

Once read, Harry regarded the youth who looked shellshocked.

"Shall we go?" replied Harry.

DS Khan lightly touched Duane's shoulder and guided him back through the snooker hall and out to the waiting police car. As he reached the car, he looked back and saw Des Daly, the snooker hall owner, in the doorway.

"I'll ring your dad, Duane. Don't sweat about a thing."

Chapter 12

London 2017

Michael 'Mick' Lange sat at the bar in a pub called the Tortoise and Hare near Oxford Street sipping on a whisky.

He had been back in London a week after looking up an old army buddy and dossing down on his sofa.

After being discharged from the army, he had flown immediately out to Spain to visit his Aunt Sarah who had married a Spaniard ten years ago and lived in Malaga in the south of the country. They owned half a dozen holiday villas and had a nice little business going.

Aunt Sarah had been the sister of Mick's mother Emily. As a youngster, Sarah would look after him in the summer holidays because his parents were always working. Sarah had then lived in the seaside resort of Weston-super-Mare, some twenty-five miles from his home in Bristol. He had many a fond memory of the place.

Sarah didn't judge and had an easy-going nature about her which Mick loved. He had stayed close to her after his parents had died in a car crash on the M5 coming back from London on a stormy November's night.

Mick had just begun his army training when the accident occurred, and he was allowed home on compassionate leave for the funeral. Thrown back into training immediately, he never really had time to grieve for his parents. The last time he had spoken to them when they were alive was an argument about him signing up to military life.

Both his parents were devout Catholics and spent a lot of their time involved in church activities. They were both pacifists and detested violence. They were never going to see eye to eye with young Mick.

His Aunt Sarah was at the funeral and, after at the wake, had told Mick to stay in touch wherever he went. She would always be there for him.

He had done this during his military travels, writing her regular letters which she always answered. He looked forward to receiving them.

On coming out of the army, she was the first person he rang. She was over the moon to hear from him and said that he was most welcome to visit and stay in one of the villas.

Mick went out there for rest and recuperation in the beautiful, warm climate. In between time spent with Sarah and her husband Agustin. Both were now in their late seventies, but the climate had served them well. They were both fit and spritely for their age.

Michael ran on the beach and swam in the sea every day. He also joined a local gym.

He stayed out in Spain for three months. The sun felt good on his skin. He loved the lifestyle, but knew that he would have to return to England soon.

His recovery went well. He was feeling fit and strong again. His hearing had returned. The bullet wounds had healed, as had his leg, although he still walked with a slight limp.

He headed back to the UK with a promise to his aunt that he would return soon.

Mick felt that he was now ready for his new mission in life, but was waiting for a sign from God to tell him where to go and what to do. After all, the world was filled with evil that needed to be eradicated, but where did he start?

He was now Michael the Archangel. God had told him so. He was more than ready to fulfil his role. But God had not spoken to him since he had been in hospital.

The night he decided to have a drink in the Tortoise and Hare was the night that he got his first sign.

* * *

Mick Lange left the bar that night and walked out into the cool night air. He lit up a cigarette.

That is when he saw a man and woman having an argument. It was heated. At first, it just looked like a couple who had too much to drink letting off steam. But when Mick went to walk off, he heard the woman let out a piercing scream.

He looked back and saw the man punching the woman to the ground and then kicking her in the stomach. Mick immediately ran over to help her. As he got closer, he realised to his horror that the woman was heavily pregnant.

The man was oblivious to Mick's presence. He was grunting with exhaustion from kicking the cowering woman.

"You fucking bitch. I know that's not my kid. You've been fucking around, you whore."

Mick closed in.

"Hey! Stop that now! You're going to kill her!" he shouted.

The man turned around momentarily. His face was a mask of rage.

"Fuck off, pal. This is none of your business."

He went back to kicking.

Mick shouted even louder.

"I said, stop it right now!"

This seemed to get through to the man as he spun around and pulled a knife from his pocket.

"I told you to fuck off."

Mick eyed the blade warily and replied.

"I can't do that."

The man smiled.

"Well, in that case, you're fucking dead."

He lunged forward, thrusting the blade towards Mick's torso.

Mick moved to the outside of the man's knife arm and parried it, before grabbing the wrist tight. He brought his forearm upwards in a smashing blow to the man's elbow, dislocating it and sending the knife flying.

He could have left it there, but an anger was rising inside of him as he regarded the woman lying bleeding on the pavement.

From dislocating the man's elbow, Mick stomped down through his knee, ripping the ligaments as the man fell forward. He then moved behind the man, wrapped his arm around his throat and squeezed tightly. The man flailed wildly trying to break the hold, but it was futile.

A small crowd had now gathered, but Mick didn't register them. Suddenly, he was back in Afghanistan. This man was Taliban. The enemy. He had to die.

Mick squeezed harder.

Suddenly, the man's thrashing ceased.

When he slid to the pavement, he was already dead.

Mick stood frozen to the spot.

He was still there when the police turned up and arrested him.

* * *

Mick Lange was convicted of manslaughter after the beaten woman testified that if he hadn't intervened, she feared that her and her baby would have died.

He was sentenced to eight years in Wandsworth Prison.

His identity and past were found out.

The army, however, had washed their hands of him and didn't want to get involved with an ex-SAS captain. They didn't want the publicity. Lange was now a civilian. He was on his own.

So, he went to prison.

Mick Lange, or Michael as he now wanted to be called, was a model prisoner. He kept his nose clean and towed the line.

Prison was not unlike the army. It was all about routine and discipline. Michael could do that standing on his head.

He knew that he had to get out of prison as soon as possible to carry on his work.

Michael began to read the Bible every day and attended Sunday mass in the prison chapel.

Then, one night, God had come to him in a vision while he lay on his bed in his cell. He told him that, when he got released, he should go back to his home city of Bristol, look up the relatives of Joe Eccles and put those ghosts to rest, before he began his mission there.

God said other angels were doing the same across the world in a race against time to save humanity. The clock was ticking on when humanity would destroy themselves unless drastic action was taken.

Greed, hate and selfishness had taken hold of a big percentage of the human race. Life was cheap. Morals, ethics and respect had gone down the drain. The beautiful world he had created was rapidly falling apart. Those who were destroying it needed to be answerable.

He told Michael that he had sent coronavirus as a warning to mankind to change their selfish ways. It had worked for a while, but now it had gone back to how it was before.

Throughout time, he had sent similar plagues and diseases as warnings, but nothing ever changed.

The time for a loving arm to be wrapped around humanity was gone. Now, evil had to be handled with an iron fist.

* * *

Michael was released after five years for good behaviour. With the help of the probation service, he got a job washing up in a restaurant, which resulted in him earning enough to get a bedsit.

Once deemed settled by the authority, he was cut loose of the system again and once more went off grid.

That's when he headed for Bristol.

He arrived in October 2023 to begin his campaign of soul taking.

Chapter 13

Duane sat in interview room one at the Temple Police HQ. Across the table from him were DCI Bowe and DS Khan.

Next to Duane was Larry McGinn, Charlie Rawlings' solicitor and brief.

As soon as Charlie had received the phone call from Des Daly, he was on the phone to McGinn and then on his way to the police station.

Charlie Rawlings was now in the reception area, prowling up and down like a caged lion. He had told McGinn to get his son out of custody asap.

DCI Bowe started the tape recording and did all the introductions.

"Right, Duane. It's simple. I know you were at the Patels and I know you were the instigator of the robbery."

Duane smirked.

"No comment."

"CCTV footage confirms you were outside with your mates."

"No comment."

"Your mates got battered by a stranger who intervened during the robbery and, by the look of your face, so did you," continued Harry.

"No comment."

"Your admission about the bat earlier has already dropped you in the shit."

Duane looked at the ceiling, smiling.

"No comment."

Harry now leant forward.

"But worse than all that, your mate Craig has owned up to the stabbing. To lighten his sentence, he gave you up as being there at the scene."

The smirk suddenly disappeared from his face.

"He wouldn't do that."

It was Harry's turn to smile.

"I thought that might get your attention. When I told him that, with this new clampdown on knife crime, he was looking at ten years maximum, he started singing like a canary."

Duane looked towards McGinn for advice.

McGinn was also looking rattled by this latest disclosure.

Harry pressed harder.

"Now, as much as I would like to see you behind bars for a long time, I have bigger fish to fry. So, let's cut to the chase. Tell me as much as you know about your attacker and I can make this sentence lighter for you. You'll be back on the streets in no time and you can tell your buddies how you gave the Old Bill the runaround. You carry on with the 'no comment' route and I can't help you. Neither can your brief here or your dad. You will do time."

Harry saw fear flicker in the young man's eyes.

McGinn saw it too.

"I suggest you say nothing at this stage. I would..."

Duane cut in.

"Alright. I'll tell you what I know, but we have a deal, right?"

Harry nodded.

"Yes. We have a deal."

Duane pulled his chair up tighter to the table.

"He was a big dude, 6' plus, solid build. He was dressed head to toe in black. He had a black beard. He was confident. Didn't show any fear, like he was used to violence."

"Accent?" asked DS Khan.

Duane thought for a moment.

"Not sure. Maybe Bristolian, but not from my neighbourhood."

"Have you ever seen him before?"

Duane shook his head. Then, there was silence.

"Is that it?" asked Harry.

"That's it, man. It all happened so fast. I didn't get a chance to take a photo," replied Duane.

Harry's gaze bore into the younger man.

"I'll need more than that if we're going to strike a deal."

Duane sat back in frustration.

"What can I tell you, man? That's it."

"Tattoos? Distinguishing marks? Branded clothing? Fucking aftershave?" asked DS Khan.

"Not that I was aware of."

Harry stood up and paced the room.

"Think. This man is dangerous. We need to get him off the streets."

Duane shrugged his shoulders. Then, he seemed to have a light bulb moment.

"Wait. There was something else. A smell."

Harry sat down again.

"Go on."

"When he was up close to me, his coat smelt of…"

Duane tried to find the words.

"What is that stuff hippies burn? They use it in yoga as well."

"You mean josh sticks?"

"Sort of, but it didn't have those sickly smells. It smelt like a church."

"You mean incense?"

"Yeah, that's it. I remember at school as a young kid having to go to mass and they were always burning the stuff. Yeah, it was incense."

Harry chewed this over for a moment.

He then looked at his watch.

He logged the time and ended the interview.

"Did that help? Are we square?" asked Duane.

Harry stood up, tidied up his paperwork and put it inside a manila file.

"Yes. We're straight."

He then looked to the constable stood by the door.

"Okay. Take Mr Rawlings back to his cell. Mr McGinn, you have twenty minutes with him to have a chat."

* * *

When DCI Bowe walked out to reception, Charlie Rawlings was right on him.

"Where's my boy? What have you fuckers set him up with?"

Harry put his hands up.

"Okay, Charlie. Take it easy. The boy is in trouble, but he's cooperated with us, so that'll be noted in court. He'll appear tomorrow in court. I expect he'll make bail and be home with you by teatime."

"Can I see him?" asked Rawlings, his voice now losing its aggressive tone.

"I'll see what I can do. Take a seat."

Rawlings looked at Harry for a moment.

"Do you know who this fucker that did him over is?"

"At this stage, no. But even if I did, I'm not going to tell you, am I?"

"I'll find him and he'll pay with his life."

"I'll pretend I didn't hear that, Charlie, but another outburst like that and I'll put you in a cell to cool down."

Charlie Rawlings glared at the DCI and then walked back to a row of plastic chairs and sat down. His day really wasn't going well.

***

At 4:00pm sharp, Harry was in the incident room with the rest of the team. He filled them in on the arrest of Duane Rawlings and what the youth had told them. He also spoke about his conversation with DS Hart.

"Incense?" mused Jim Leech, "That's weird. What is this guy then? A priest or something?"

"I don't know, Jim, but I think it would be worth us checking out churches in the area."

Leech nodded and made a note on his pad.

Harry continued.

"DS Hart got back to me. He went through CCTV outside the Patels. Again, the cameras aren't positioned great, but we did pick up four youths on bikes in the park across the way from the shop. Their images tie up with the descriptions the Patels gave us."

"Any images of them or anybody else going in or out the shop?" asked Leech.

"Afraid not, sir. There's no camera directly on the premises," answered Rose, "We did, however, catch a glimpse of a black transit van turning the corner next to the Patel's, but couldn't pick up a registration or the driver. It might be something."

"Go back to Dawn Little and see if she remembers a black transit van at the scene of the murders," said Harry.

He now looked back to Jim.

"Any luck at the Jungle Club?"

Leech consulted his notes.

"The manager, Terry Stone, was most helpful. He let me and Bailey look at CCTV footage from the night of the murders. We clearly see the three murdered doormen talking to a passing Dawn Little around 1:30am and then, ten minutes later, we see Tony Ellis leave the door and walk in the direction Dawn had headed. About another ten minutes later, White and Comer disappear from the door too. We also kept checking the passersby after Dawn had walked off and bingo, we found this dude. The description fits what Dawn Little and the Patels told us.

Jim pinned a large black and white photo up on the murder board.

"He only appears fleetingly on camera before moving out of range, but I think it's our boy."

Harry and the rest of the team regarded it.

"Is that the best image we can get?" asked Harry.

Jim nodded.

"That's it, guv."

"Did the actual video throw up anything new?" questioned DS French.

"Yes, it did. The man walks with a pronounced limp on his left leg. You can clearly see it."

"Good man, Jim. Now that is something new and something positive to go on," said Harry, "The limp is a significant breakthrough. He might be able to hide his face from the cameras, but not the limp."

"Just asking, sir. If it is the suspect, wouldn't Dawn Little and the Patels have noticed the limp and mentioned it?" asked DC Kenny Stewart.

"Good point. Any thoughts?"

Harry opened the question to the room.

DS Rose was right on it.

"Not necessarily. Dawn Little told us she was curled up in the back of the transit when the man spoke to her and when she looked up, he was already gone. In the case of Patels, everything happened so fast and so brutally, I think they were both in trauma and probably didn't notice. Mrs Patel, who had the best look at the man, was probably more concerned with her husband's health after the stabbing."

"Agreed," said Harry, "In the case of Duane Rawlings and his buddies, they were too occupied having the shit beat out of them to notice."

He then pointed to the photograph.

"So, we go with the assumption this could well be our killer. Anything more?"

DS Rose cut in.

"You're going to like this, guv. I went to the Pacifica nightclub and looked at their CCTV footage. I found Dawn Little leaving the club. But more interestingly, we also picked up this guy. I believe that is the same man that Jim picked up outside the Jungle Club. Same clothes and build, and he has a limp."

DS Rose pinned her photo image to the board next to the other one. Both men looked identical.

"We have recordings of both of these sightings, right?" asked Harry.

"Yes, guv," both Leech and Rose confirmed.

DC Sharma entered the room and handed Harry a large manila envelope. Harry opened it and produced the forensic sketch. It joined the other evidence on the board.

"This is a sketch done of our proposed killer from the descriptions we were given. It will be on the front of the tabloids tomorrow morning. Somebody somewhere must have some clue who it might be. With this image and the CCTV footage we've captured, I believe we're looking at the killer."

Everybody in the room regarded the images in silence.

"Tomorrow, DS Rose and DC Sharma, your next task is to chat to Dawn Little about a black transit. DS Leech and DC Bailey, check out local churches. See if anybody going there may fit our man's description. Again, it's a long shot, but worth a try. DS French, keep the board updated and man the phones. DC Stewart, hit the streets for your duties and keep your eyes open. DS Khan, you're with me. We'll pay a visit to the Vault Gym."

"Sir, just to conclude..." said DS French, "As you requested, I put out feelers to other police departments in major cities within a 100-mile radius to see if our man may have been active there as well. So far no luck, but I'll keep digging."

"Thanks, Carrie," replied Harry.

* * *

When the meeting was over, Harry rang Tommy Good and gave him the update. He told him that this was the last piece of exclusive news as Superintendent Bradley had called a press conference for 14:00pm the next day to inform all media sources on the latest news.

Harry added that he would swing around to 'Goodie' in the morning with printouts of CCTV footage photos and copies of the sketch. He wanted them circulated all over Bristol.

Harry made it home for a proper dinner with Carol and a chance to have a catch up. It had been sometime since this had happened. Carol told Harry about her day at the hospital.

He had never known a person so dedicated to helping and caring for people. It was as if she had been put on this planet just for that reason. A proper little Florence Nightingale.

In times of COVID-19, she had seen some horrific things, but she never once complained and just kept on working helping save lives throughout it all.

Through their jobs, both of them carried many mental scars, but as long as they had each other to sound off of, they could cope.

Harry loved her dearly and promised himself that he would take her away for a nice break as soon as he put this killer behind bars.

Over a dinner of lamb casserole, Carol reminded him to go and visit his mother with her Christmas present. She was ninety years of age and lived in a care home, but was still as sharp as a tack.

He had spoken to her the previous week on the phone when he asked her what she wanted for Christmas.

She had told him the new Iphone15 or Tom Cruise. He still wasn't sure if she had been joking.

Carol then spoke about plans for Christmas.

They were going to her sister Sarah's house for lunch. She lived in Gloucester around about forty miles away from Bristol.

Harry liked Sarah, but her husband Rodney was a pompous prick. He was a chef and a right sanctimonious one at that. He made Gordon Ramsey seem like Ainsley Harriet.

Sarah and Rodney came to Harry's house last year and, after one too many brandies, Rodney decided to spout off about all that was wrong with the police. Harry had resisted the temptation not to punch his lights out.

Sarah had hastily ordered a taxi to get him home.

Christmas. A time of peace and joy to all men.

All the talk of the festive season made him realise that he needed to start thinking himself about buying some presents.

He was forever leaving it to the last minute.

But the dark spectre of the killer was casting a shadow over the coming festive period.

Harry and Carol finished the evening off by taking their glasses of red wine into the living room and watching a film, which they both nodded off to halfway through. However, when they finally made it to bed, Harry found it difficult to sleep as thoughts of the case came rushing back into his mind.

At 2:58am, his phone pinged. Harry reached for it with a feeling of dread in his stomach.

He saw it was DS Rose.

When he answered, his greatest fears came true.

The killer had struck again.

Chapter 14

Michael had been waiting for some time. The night was cold, but he ignored the sub-zero temperature and the flakes of snow falling as he had a job to do.

He watched the house and had waited for the lights to finally go out. That had been half an hour ago.

He decided it was time to make his move.

The property was rented to a Janet Carey through social housing; she shared it with her boyfriend Marvin Crook. Janet also had a three-month-old daughter named Jasmine.

Social services had visited the house on more than one occasion, suspecting the baby was being neglected and physically abused. The house had also been visited by police due to neighbours complaining about blazing rows and screaming and crying.

Janet had sported a black eye or a cut lip more than once.

Crook was a vicious thug and a drug user.

To Michael, he was the scum of the earth. A lowlife who had to pay for his crimes.

He had been delivered his name.

The police and the authorities were going to do nothing until both mother and child would be found dead.

Michael couldn't let that happen.

He now walked towards the house and checked nobody was around.

It was 2:00am and all was quiet.

Crook's pride and joy was sat outside the front of the house. A white BMW grand coupe sport. Michael walked up to it and picked up a heavy stone from the front garden rockery. He then hauled it with as much force as he could muster through the driver's side window. Immediately, the alarm sounded, splitting the quiet of the night.

Michael crouched in the front garden behind the bushes.

Lights went on in the house and a baby started to cry.

Marvin Crook stood at the bedroom window and pulled back the curtains. He looked down at his car, all flashing lights and noise.

"Some fucker is trying to break into my motor!" he shouted.

Janet clutched her daughter and said nothing. When Marvin lost it, there was no talking to him.

"I'll fucking have the bastard," he added as he opened the wardrobe and took out a Samurai sword.

He unsheathed it and ran out the bedroom dressed in just his boxers.

He ran down the stairs, out through the front door and down the garden path towards his car. He was so angry that he didn't register the cold.

Michael had been betting on the fact that, if Crook had been woken from his sleep, he would react with his heart and not his head.

"Come on, you pussy. Where are you? Come out if you have the balls!" screamed Crook.

Lights in nearby houses went on, alerted by the noise.

Michael knew that he didn't have much time.

He stepped out from the bushes, moved silently up to Crook, slipped a thin cord around his neck and pulled tightly. Crook reacted by having to drop the sword that he was carrying and reach up for the ligature.

Michael drove his knee into the base of the man's spine and pulled tighter. Crook started convulsing and his limbs twitched uncontrollably as he was starved of precious oxygen.

Michael now turned his back to the man, drove his hips into his lower back and bent forward. Crook's feet were lifted from the ground and the force of the cord on his throat now became a hangman's noose.

The man's last movements were futile.

He was dead.

Michael released the cord and Crook's body slumped to the concrete.

Michael stepped in close and spoke.

"May God have mercy on your soul or the devil will take it."

Michael walked away quickly and disappeared down the road.

Two streets away, he found his transit van.

He jumped into it, started it up and headed into the night.

Another mission accomplished and another of society's dredges brought to judgement.

* * *

Harry and Diane Rose sat in a squad car sipping coffee. Across the road, the body of Marvin Crook was being finally loaded in the coroner's van. The area was sealed off, but still a hive of activity.

Doctor Brendan Daly had confirmed death was by strangulation using a thin ligature, probably a cord of some sort. Time of death was roughly 2:00-2:30am.

The victim was attacked from behind and had no time to use the weapon he had supposedly been brandishing: the samurai sword.

Death had been swift and, once again, expertly executed.

Crook was known to Harry.

He was a nasty piece of work and, in the big scheme of things, he would not be missed by many.

It certainly made life easier for the police with the piece of scum out the way, but the problem for Bowe and his team now was that they had no doubt they were dealing with a vigilante and they couldn't conceal that fact any longer.

The press conference later today was going to be a powder keg.

"Anybody see what happened?" asked Harry, already knowing the answer.

This neighbourhood wasn't going to give the police anything.

"No, sir. Not of much use. A Mr and Mrs Bennett next door heard glass smash and a car alarm go off around 2:00am. That in itself is not unusual in this neighbourhood. Mr Bennett said he got up to check it wasn't his car. The driveway of the deceased can't be seen from the Bennetts' bedroom. Mr Bennett presumed it was Marvin Crook's car, but couldn't see anything. He did add, though, that he didn't – in his words – 'give a fuck about the piece of shit'."

Harry nodded.

"What about the girlfriend?"

"She said that she was frightened when Crook ran out with the sword, so she stayed with her daughter in bed. When he hadn't returned after ten minutes, she looked out of the bedroom window and saw his body on the drive and called us. She saw nobody else."

Harry slammed his palm down on the dashboard in frustration.

"Nothing again. This guy is just randomly popping up and murdering people. There's no visible pattern to the killings."

DS Rose nodded.

"I agree, sir. But as random as the killings may be, this man knows exactly what he's doing. These murders are planned. They're not unorganised or frenzied. This is somebody used to doing this stuff. I definitely think he's ex-military."

"If he is, that would be like looking for a needle in a haystack. There are thousands of ex-military back in 'civvies'. We need a clear photo image or description to go with the fact that he limps on his left leg. Then – and only then – would we have a hope of identifying this man through army records. The killer must have got away in a vehicle. If the black transit van is his, then maybe CCTV has picked it up parked somewhere nearby. Check this out as soon as you can later this morning," said Harry.

DS Rose looked at her boss. He looked tired.

"What now?"

"Home for a few hours, then back in the office at 9:00am to follow on the leads we had from yesterday's meeting and the latest ones."

Harry started the car. As he pulled away, DS Rose spoke.

"I expect the Super will be on your case first thing when he hears the news."

Harry sighed.

"I can hardly wait."

* * *

After he dropped DS Rose at her home, he drove to police HQ. He knew he wouldn't be able to sleep. His mind was in a whirl.

He had texted Carol telling her not to expect him back any time soon.

Harry got himself a coffee and sat at his desk.

He did this often, coming into work in the wee small hours.

When the place was not a hubbub of industry, he could think better.

Apart from who was this killer, the burning questions he wanted answered were how did the killer select his victims and how did he know where to find them?

He still had a gut feeling about Diane Rose's theory that he could be a member of the Vault Gym. It was a haven for the criminal world. Harry wondered if the latest victim, Marvin Crook, had used the gym. He would definitely visit it tomorrow morning.

The incense thing bothered him too. Was it just a red herring or did it mean more than that?

Harry now walked into the incident room and studied the murder board. He scrutinised the black and white images of what could be the killer. He was an imposing figure, but the black outfit and beanie hat gave nothing more away about him. The limp was a significant clue, however.

Tomorrow, the whole media would know all the gory details of the murders, including the latest one.

Suddenly, Harry felt bone weary.

He switched off his desk lamp and walked over to the sofa in the corner of his office. He opened up a cabinet next to it and pulled out a blanket.

Harry settled down on the sofa and checked his watch. It read 4:15am. He set an alarm on his phone for 7:00am.

This time, he was asleep as soon as his head touched the cushion.

Chapter 15

Next morning at 9:00am sharp, Harry and DS Khan phoned Tommy Good to confirm that the press conference would be at 14:00pm.

Harry also told 'Goodie' his suspicions about the Vault Gym and that he was on his way there now to investigate them. He promised that he would fill him in before the press conference if he turned anything up.

As soon as Harry finished the call, his phone rang again.

It was Superintendent Bradley.

Harry addressed it immediately as he didn't want the man ringing him on and off all morning.

"Morning, sir."

"Morning, Harry. Just checking you have all you need for the press conference. You know the press will be baying for blood and, no disrespect, but I don't want it to be mine."

Harry rolled his eyes.

"Don't worry, sir. We have everything in order. I'm just on my way to the Vault Gym to follow up another promising lead."

This seemed to satisfy Bradley.

"Okay. Good. See you this afternoon."

A text now came through to Harry from DS Rose, informing him that she had rang Dawn Little and she doesn't remember any other van apart from the white one she had been pushed into.

Another dead end.

* * *

At 9:40am, Harry and DS Khan pulled up outside the Vault Gym.

"Right, we need to get some information out of Mr Lyons. The more leads I can take to Bradley and then the press conference, the better. I know I'm going to be grilled and, as head of this investigation, I know I'll also be hung out to dry if I don't get a major break in the case soon."

DS Khan empathised with his boss. He had known Harry for some years and knew he was a good copper. Straight as an arrow and always ready to give 100% to the job. He had solved some tough cases in his time, but Khan also knew that you were only as good as your last arrest.

The two men entered the gym and headed for reception. They immediately saw the man who had told DS Rose previously that he was called Arnold Schwarzenegger.

He was reading the newspaper and looked up when he spotted them.

"Yes, can I help you?"

"We'd like a word with the owner Ed Lyons."

The man now eyed them suspiciously as he lowered the newspaper.

"And who might you be then?"

Harry and Khan both flashed their warrant cards.

"DCI Harry Bowe and DS Ali Khan," announced Harry.

The man smirked.

"Did you say Harry Bowe?"

Before he could continue, Harry interrupted.

"I've heard all the sweet jokes, so don't waste your breath. Who might you be?"

The man folded his paper and put it down.

"Gerry Tucker. I do a bit of reception work here."

"Can you get your boss, please? This is important," said Harry.

The cocky smirk disappeared from the man's face as he rose from his stool. He flexed his chest and biceps in a show of intimidation.

"I'll see if he's about."

* * *

Minutes later, Ed Lyons appeared.

"Yes, gentlemen. How can I help?"

"Are you the owner of this gym, Ed Lyons?" asked Harry.

"Yes, I am."

Harry continued.

"Two of my officers came around here the other day and I believe they spoke with your daughter who told them she wasn't in authority to let us see your membership files."

"That's right, officers. Private and confidential. Have you a warrant?"

Harry deliberately ignored the question.

"There was recently the murders of three men who used your gym. Tony Ellis, Chris Comer and Errol White."

Lyons nodded.

"Yes, terrible business. A shocker. You caught anybody for it yet?"

"This is what we're looking into, Mr Lyons, and we could do with your help," replied DS Khan, "Can I ask if a Marvin Crook used the gym?"

Ed looked thoughtful.

"Yeah. Sometimes. I haven't seen him for a while though. Why?"

"Because he was also murdered in the early hours of this morning."

Lyons looked genuinely shocked.

"Shit. That's terrible. But I know nothing about it. I can't help you."

Harry moved closer to the counter.

"Mr Lyons, I was hoping we could do this the easy way, but you're leaving me no choice. Four men of dodgy reputations have been found murdered and all were members of your gym. Doesn't that set alarm bells ringing? Now, this gym has got a certain reputation for – shall we say – some shady characters hanging out here. On that evidence, I could go get a warrant and also a drugs team with sniffer dogs in here just to see what they might turn up, but that is a lot of fuss and paperwork. All I want to know is has anybody new joined the gym in the last few months?"

Lyons shifted uncomfortably behind the counter.

"It's been quiet recently, especially since that new gym opened across town with its special fucking offers. I've been losing members, not gaining them."

"Anybody else come in here or been hanging around?" asked DS Khan.

Lyons shook his head.

"No. Well, except the guy I took on as a cleaner. He came in looking for a few hours of work, cash in hand, and as our regular cleaner had just left, I took him on."

Harry and Ali Khan exchanged glances.

"What's this man's name?" asked Harry.

"Michael. I only know him as Michael. I know nothing else about him," replied Lyons, "Like I said, he was a handy stop gap between employing a proper cleaner."

Harry felt an explosion of adrenaline hit his belly.

He pulled up the image of the sketch on his phone and showed it to Lyons.

"Is this him?"

Lyons looked at the image.

"Yes. It's a decent likeness."

"Is he here now?"

Lyons nodded.

"Yes. I was just chatting to him before I came out to see you. He was cleaning the showers."

"Show me to him now, and quick!" said Harry.

* * *

Bowe, Khan and Lyons headed for the changing rooms. Harry pushed open the door and surveyed the room.

There were two men dressing in there and there was a bucket and mop in the centre of the floor. The doors to the two shower cubicles were closed. DS Khan walked over to the cubicles and cautiously pushed them both open. They were empty.

Lyons now regarded the two men.

"The cleaner that was in here, do you know where he went?"

The man straightening his tie in the mirror replied.

"He was here cleaning the floor a few minutes ago and then he answered his phone. Next thing I know he was out of here like his ass was on fire. Maybe his missus has gone into labour?"

Harry and Khan ran out of the changing rooms and down the corridor. They saw a fire door swinging open to a car park beyond. Both of them ran to the door just in time to catch a glimpse of a black transit van roaring out of the gates. It was going too quick to pick up the number plate.

DS Khan pulled out his radio and ordered an APB on a black transit going at speed in or around the vicinity of the Vault Gym. He added 'approach with caution, dangerous subject'.

Lyons caught up with the two policemen.

Harry eyed him steely.

"If, for any reason, he comes back here, I want to know, day or night. Understand?"

Lyons nodded as he took the card Harry handed to him.

He then asked.

"What has he done?"

Harry knew he had to tell this man, so that he would take the whole situation seriously.

"We believe he may have been responsible for the deaths of Ellis, Comer and White, as well as Crooks and others."

"Jesus!" exclaimed Lyons, "He seemed decent enough. Quiet and reserved certainly, but I would never have him down for a fucking psycho."

"Well, now you know. You or any of your gym members could be next. So, keep an eye out for him and report straight to me."

"Okay. Okay. Understood," said Lyons.

DS Khan now spoke.

"Does this Michael character have a locker here? Somewhere he might store anything of a personal nature during working hours?"

"Yes. I gave him the key to number 7 locker," answered Lyons.

"Show us where it is."

* * *

The three men stood in front of number 7 locker. As suspected, it was locked shut.

"You have a spare key?" asked Harry.

"Yes. I'll go and get it now."

Lyons moved off.

Once he was out of earshot, Harry spoke.

"Shit, I don't believe we were that close to him. DS Rose's suspicion about the gym proved right."

"Also, the black transit appearing again. It's got to be his," added Khan.

"Let's hope they can track it. That would be a major breakthrough," added Harry.

"Yes, seeing Rose came up blank when she spoke to Dawn Little."

Harry looked thoughtful.

"The phone call this Michael received that caused him to rush off... do you think somebody tipped him off we were coming to the gym?"

"Like who, guv? How would anybody know?"

"Um... seems strange. One minute, he's cleaning and the next, he's gone like a rabbit.

Lyons returned with the key and opened the locker.

Inside was a black, battered Adidas sports bag.

Lyons went to take it out, but Harry grabbed his wrist.

"Evidence, Mr Lyons. We'll take it from here."

DS Khan slipped on a pair of surgical gloves and took the bag out. He checked the locker again, but that was all that was inside it. Harry also slipped on gloves and they took the bag to a nearby table.

They carefully unzipped the bag. Inside, they found a clean t-shirt and tracksuit bottoms.

"Did he work out here?" asked Harry.

"Well, I gave him a free membership, but I don't recall seeing him training myself. That's not to say he didn't. I'm not here 24/7," answered Lyons.

Further inspection of the bag produced a plastic water bottle, which was empty.

"With any luck, that should produce some DNA and maybe some fingerprints," said Khan.

In a side-zipped pocket, Khan found a small book. On inspection, it was a Bible.

On the inside cover was a handwritten inscription: *For Michael, a gift from your friend Father Matthew.*

"Bingo. We've unearthed some hard evidence," exclaimed Harry.

On inspection of the Bible, Khan found a highlighted passage.

It was from the Book of Revelations 12:7: *Then war broke out in heaven; and his angels battled against the dragon. The dragon and its angels fought back, but they did not prevail and there was no longer any place for them in heaven.*

"Know what that means?" asked Harry.

Khan half smiled.

"Wrong religion for me, guv."

Harry glanced at Lyons, who immediately put both hands up and shook his head.

"Right, let's get SOCO in here to examine the locker and to get the bag to the lab asap. This is a major breakthrough and right on time for the press conference."

Harry now regarded Lyons.

"We'll require you to shut off the changing rooms until SOCO have done their job."

Lyons nodded.

"I'll tell members that there's a water leak in there. Your boys can come through the backway and not through the gym. I have a reputation to uphold here, you know."

Harry smiled.

"Okay, Mr Lyons. Thank you for your cooperation. And remember, if this man returns here, I want to be first to know."

Harry now regarded DS Khan.

"Remain here, Ali, until the team have done their job. Also, ring Jim and tell him about the Bible and the name Father Matthew. That might cut his search down on the local churches."

"What would be his connection with a priest? It hardly seems fitting," said Khan.

Harry peeled off his gloves.

"Hopefully, we'll find that out sooner rather than later. When you finish, ring HQ and get somebody to come pick you up. I have a press conference to get ready for."

Chapter 16

The press conference that was held at the civic centre initially went better than Harry had expected. He had sat at the top table, along with Superintendent Bradley and press liaison officer Jennifer Baker. She was brought in to vet or fend off any awkward questions if need be.

The room was stuffed with press and media. Flashlights were clicking and everybody present was jostling to get their questions answered.

Harry noticed Tommy Good near the back of the room. Goodie nodded in his direction.

Superintendent Bradley introduced himself, then DCI Bowe and finally Jennifer Baker. He then went on to outline the purpose of the meeting. Once finished, he turned the questioning over to the floor.

Harry knew that the Super would have his back if necessary, but he also realised that he was the leading officer and the questions would be fired at him.

Harry disclosed the new evidence, handing out images of the would-be killer and telling them about the CCTV footage from the nightclubs. He mentioned the black transit van being spotted twice so far, although earlier it had managed to elude the police. Plus, DS Rose had since confirmed that no vehicle of that description had shown up on CCTV in Crook's neighbourhood. Then, he covered the find at the gym and told them that he would keep them up to speed if DNA evidence was found.

The one thing that he kept back was the man's limp. This was a personal piece of information that he wanted to withhold for now. If somebody rang in to police HQ either claiming to be the killer or saying that they knew him, this crucial piece of evidence would determine the genuine from the fakers and looney tunes that loved to waste police time.

Superintendent Bradley then took centre stage to give an update on the latest murder victim Marvin Crook and the manner he had died. The press asked if it was definitely the same MO as the previous killings and whether they were sure it was the same man, given that a knife had not been used.

Bradley confirmed that, although a knife had not been used, the cold and clinical way that the man had been dispatched pointed to the same killer.

Then, Tommy Good asked the big question.

"Superintendent, can you confirm if we are dealing with a vigilante?"

Bradley suddenly felt a little hot under the collar.

"I can neither confirm nor deny this at the present moment."

"So, you need another lowlife murdered before you can be sure. Is that what you're saying?" replied Good.

Bradley glanced at Harry and DCI saw the look of concern on his boss's face.

He decided to intervene.

Harry was pissed off that Goodie had decided to take centre stage in the conference and bring up the question, but he knew from the past that Tommy Good loved an audience and his burning ambition to be editor of one of the main national newspapers overrode caution.

"What we have, Tom, is a killer. *Who* he is killing is not as important as *why*."

"That may be so, Detective Inspector, but is it not a fact that all the deceased were criminals?"

"Yes, that's correct, but we're more concerned that there are deaths on the streets of Bristol and we need to stop them. I believe, with the evidence we've uncovered today, we're a step nearer to doing so. I think the public will be heartened by this news."

Good smiled and nodded.

"True, Inspector. But don't you think the public should know that there's a vigilante out on their streets? I believe members of the public have already expressed the opinion that, rather than these murders deterring them from walking out on the streets at night, they indeed feel safer now that the man who we're now calling 'The Avenging Angel' is out there."

Harry felt an overriding urge to go down into the assembled throng and punch Goodie's lights out, but he pushed the feeling down.

"There is no hard evidence to suggest that this is what the public think. I am confident that we'll have this man in custody soon."

Goodie went to speak again, but Jennifer Baker intervened.

"I'm afraid that's all the time we have, ladies and gentlemen of the press. Thank you for coming."

With that, she left the room, closely followed by Bradley and Bowe.

* * *

In the corridor outside, Harry caught up with Tom Good and guided him by the arm without ceremony into the Gents washroom. Once inside, he pushed the man away.

"What the fuck are you playing at, busting my ass out there? I thought we had an understanding."

"Yeah, we have an understanding, Harry. We both mutually help each other," replied Goodie.

"Well, enlighten me. How did that help me earlier?" asked Harry.

Goodie's face broke into a smile.

"Hey, Harry. All is fair in love and war. The question needed to be asked and I asked it. Look, there are some of the big tabloids out there. I have an ambition to be working for one of them. I'm not going to be editing *The Bristol Eye* for the rest of my days. So, I might have come on a little heavy, but I wanted to make an impression as an eager newshound while I could."

Harry walked forward. There was menace in his voice.

"You made an impression alright, Goodie, you fucking Judas."

Goodie looked offended.

"Come on, Harry. We've always worked on a quid pro quo basis. I scratch your back, you scratch mine. You know that. As much as I like you, this is a job and the reality of the situation is you've got a crusading serial killer running amok in your city and you haven't got a clue who it is. The people deserve to know this. I'm a reporter. I report."

"Fine, Goodie. You've made your position clear. Now, let me tell you something. This morning, I made a significant discovery, which I feel may lead me to the killer. I was going to share this information with you, but now I've decided not to. I will find this killer and bring him to justice, but your paper will have nothing to do with it. Do I make myself clear?"

Tom Good said nothing.

Harry turned and left the washroom.

* * *

When Harry got back to the station, DS Khan approached him.

"Guv, we've got news back from forensics. They didn't pull any fingerprints from the locker. They even examined the mop and bucket, but they were also clean. They have taken DNA from the water bottle though and are running it now through the computer looking for a match. They're also checking through the Bible, but that might take a bit longer."

"That's great news. Keep me updated," replied Harry.

"Also, I passed on the latest news to Jim Leech. He said that the Bible connection tied in with the Rawlings kid saying he smelt incense on the killer."

"Yes, I tend to agree with him. Thanks, Ali."

* * *

Harry went into his office and texted his team that there would be a meeting at 9:00am sharp the next day for updates.

Earlier, he had received a call from DS French. Sergeant Jack Hart had been in touch and told her that Mr Patel had taken a turn for the worst in hospital.

Possible sepsis. He had gone into a coma and things didn't look good. If he died, the youths who were involved in his stabbing would be facing a murder charge. On the strength of this, they were all rearrested and brought back into custody.

Apparently, Charlie Rawlings was going ape shit and threatening all sorts at the desk in HQ. He was threatened with being tasered if he didn't calm down. Eventually, he left, still spewing threats.

Harry told DS French to tell the desk sergeant to have Rawlings arrested if he came back and was abusive.

Harry guessed that Rawlings would kick off. Duane was his only child. Charlie wouldn't admit it, but he doted on the lad, even though he could be a liability at times. Now with Duane facing possible accessory to murder charges, he was at the end of his tether.

Harry knew Rawlings was going to kick off sooner or later. Duane and his buddies would have got away scot-free with the raid on the shop if it hadn't been for the intervention of this mystery man named Michael.

Harry also realised that he needed to find this man before Rawlings. Nobody crossed the Rawlings family without answering for it. It was the law of the jungle on these streets.

If Charlie found Michael first, there would be carnage.

* * *

At 6:00pm, Harry was getting ready to head home. He might even get an early dinner in for a change.

He had managed to squeeze in an hour's visit to see his mother and bring her in an early Christmas present.

He couldn't locate Tom Cruise, so he bought her favourite perfume.

The old woman had been in good spirits for a while, but eventually drifted off to sleep during Countdown on the television.

Harry's parents had been decent folk. His dad Reg had been a firefighter all his life and his mum Vera had been a teacher in a primary school.

His dad had died at 88, a great innings, and when his mum could no longer cope with the house, they sold it using funds to send her to Elmwood Care Home where she was still able to do most things for herself.

Harry did have a sister Josie, but she tragically died at ten years of age when she was abducted and murdered by child killer Barry Bowen in the 1980s. Before Bowen had been caught, he had murdered five other children after Josie.

It was front page news for many weeks. In recent times, a documentary had been made about Bowen and the killings for Netflix. The family never really got over their loss.

This tragic occurrence prompted a then fourteen-year-old Harry Bowe to want to join the police force when he was old enough. The memory of his sister's death spurred Harry on every day to make the streets safer and to catch people like Bowen and lock them up and throw away the key.

* * *

Harry slipped on his overcoat. It was bitterly cold outside and the forecast suggested snow again. Although Harry was no lover of snow – it always seemed to bring the country to a standstill – he thought it might just keep the killer off the streets.

Suddenly, there was a knock on the door. It opened and DS Khan appeared. He was smiling.

"Guv, we've got a hit on the DNA sample."

"Go on, Ali. Let's have it."

"It belongs to a man named Michael Lange, known as Mick. Here's the thing. He did time for manslaughter, but before that, he was discharged on medical grounds from the SAS where he was a Captain. PTSD. He was deemed no longer mentally fit for combat. He served for five years. I think this could be our man."

Harry took in the information.

"We have a photo of him?"

DS Khan opened the file he was holding and produced a photo.

"This is an image from his prison records."

Harry stared at an image of a man in his forties. He had long unkempt hair and a heavy growth of beard. His eyes were dark and piercing. It looked very much like the image that had been drawn up by the forensic sketch artist from witness descriptions.

"I don't suppose we have an address?"

"No current one. When he got out of prison, he seemed to have disappeared off the radar."

"Anything else of interest?"

"One more thing. He was born here in Bristol."

"Christ, that can't be a coincidence," exclaimed Harry.

"I agree, guv."

"There must be a reason why he's come back to Bristol to carry out these killings and we need to find out," said Harry, "Maybe he had family here?"

DS Khan nodded.

"We're looking into his army records now and seeing why exactly he was discharged. We'll check for next of kin too. Hopefully, I'll have more in the morning," said Khan.

"This is a major breakthrough, but we need to keep it quiet until we're totally sure this is our man. We don't want to spook him," said Harry.

"Understood, guv."

"Good work, Ali."

* * *

Harry walked over to the murder board and pinned up the latest photo. He studied the man.

What happened to you, Captain Michael 'Mick' Lange? What has caused you to go on this killing spree?

* * *

On the drive home, Harry's mind was working overtime. Finally, he had got the break he needed to hopefully solve this case.

He was in a good mood and stopped at the garage to buy a bottle of wine to go with dinner and a bunch of flowers for Carol.

Maybe it was going to be a good Christmas after all.

Chapter 17

Charlie Rawlings was sat in the back office of the Vault Gym, along with Ed Lyons and another man named Leroy Curtis.

Curtis was a hitman and had travelled down from the north as soon as Charlie had called him. He was a black man mountain of muscle.

Charlie had received a phone call earlier in the day from Ed Lyons. As soon as the police had left his gym, Lyons had rung Charlie and put him in the picture that the police thought his cleaner was the killer, which would also mean that he was the man to have done over Duane and his mates.

That day, Rawlings initially had to deal with the news that Duane was going to be rearrested, but now that this had happened, he was keen to find this man and punish him for what was happening to his son.

But he had gone into the police station earlier like a bull in a china shop, spitting out threats, so he knew that the Old Bill would be keeping tabs on him; hence, the phone call to Leroy Curtis. He was just the person to track this man down and kill him.

Rawlings studied the front of *The Bristol Eye* evening edition.

"So, this is what this joker looks like?" asked Charlie.

Ed took a sip of whisky.

"That's a bloody good image of this Michael who has been working here, yes."

Charlie remembered back to the other day when he almost tripped on the cleaning bucket in the gym and how he had shouted at the cleaner.

That had been the bastard. There in touching distance.

He swilled down his own whisky and refilled his glass.

"What else do you know about him?"

Ed spread his hands.

"As I told the Old Bill, nothing. He turned up here asking about a job. My cleaner had recently left, so I offered him the job for a few hours a day. The money was cash in hand and he could use the gym if he wanted. That was all. He mentioned he wasn't planning on being in Bristol too long and I said that suited me fine as it gave me a few weeks to find a full-time cleaner."

"Anything unusual about him? Anything the cops are holding back?" asked Charlie.

"The description is accurate. He's a big guy, seemed fit. Quiet, didn't say a lot. But the one thing I remember is he walked with a slight limp on his left leg," answered Ed, "Also, the police found a bag in his locker and one of the things in there was a Bible. It had a handwritten inscription inside from a Father Matthew."

"A priest?"

"I presume, yes."

Rawlings thought about this for a moment. For some reason, the name seemed familiar, but he couldn't place it.

"If, by any wild chance, he comes back here, you will tell me immediately, won't you?" said Rawlings.

"Yes, of course, Charlie. That goes without saying," replied Lyons.

"Do you think he's living rough?" asked Rawlings.

Lyons thought for a moment.

"Well, by his dress and demeanour, he certainly wasn't staying at the Grand. Maybe a hostel or bedsit."

"Or maybe staying with a friend like a priest," said Rawlings.

"Maybe," replied Lyons as he reached for the whisky bottle.

"I have a bad vibe about this guy. Just as I am bringing the Albanian crew here to Bristol and potentially setting up a deal, we get some lunatic in the city randomly slaying people and then taking out my boy. It's too much of a coincidence. Maybe somebody has sent him to put the frighteners on me and fuck up my deal?"

"Who the fuck even knew about the deal outside your crew, Charlie?" asked Lyons.

"Nobody I'm aware of. That's why it makes it worse. If it is somebody inside the firm, I'll have their blood. This time last month, things were sweet. Now, my boy is looking at a murder charge and this lunatic is trying to fuck me over."

Rawlings looked at the silent brooding figure of Leroy Curtis.

"We need to find this bastard fast and do away with him."

The black man nodded.

"If he's in the city, I'll find him, Charlie. You know my record is good."

Charlie nodded.

Curtis was good, but he also sensed that he may have met his match in this Michael character.

* * *

Michael sat on his bed with his head in his hands. It was late and the room was in darkness, except for a small bedside lamp casting a watery yellow glow.

He had been lucky as far as the police were concerned.

The phone tipoff had saved his ass, but he knew by now that the police must have found his bag in the gym locker and were testing the contents for DNA.

He now cursed himself for bringing it to the gym, but he needed to bring something with him. Otherwise, it might have drawn suspicion. A kit bag seemed the right call. The Bible maybe was a mistake. They would soon find out who he was and his past. The Bible given to him by Father Matthew would eventually lead them here.

He had been fortunate to get away from the gym in his van before any police vehicles had responded and gave chase, but it had been too close for comfort. His contact had told him that the policeman leading the case was dogged and would not give up.

It was time to soon leave Bristol, but his work was not quite complete. He had one more job to do. He hoped he would get time to do it. It would have to be tonight.

His target was an Asian man named Muhammad Jarwar. Jarwar and four friends were suspected of grooming underage girls for sex. They would make contact with them and promise their target the latest phones, clothing, cosmetics etc. There would also be hints of modelling or TV work. Once reeled in by their subterfuge, they would be plied with alcohol and cocaine and used as sex slaves by them and their friends.

Jarwar had been arrested twice, but evaded any prosecution by having a very sharp lawyer and a lack of concrete evidence. Jarwar was a violent and dangerous man. None of his victims would dare speak out against him, which made it nigh-on impossible for the police to prosecute him.

Michael had been given an address where Jarwar and his cronies may be hanging out. He was ready to dish out his own brand of justice to these men.

Moving to the corner of his room, he pulled back a threadbare rug and then used a tablespoon to prise up a loose concrete paving slab from the floor. Under it was a decent sized hole.

He reached in and pulled out a sack. Michael now emptied the contents out onto the floor.

There were three different combat knives. The Japanese tanto, the Fairbairn-Sykes combat dagger and a Gerber MK11. Each one was a precision piece of engineering with the prime purpose of killing.

Then, there was a Glock 17 and six ammo clips, as well as a Browning automatic 9mm, also with six ammo clips. Both guns were in shoulder holsters.

Michael checked both guns and chose the Glock 17. The gun held a clip of 17 rounds. He put on the shoulder holster and put two extra clips in his coat pocket.

He also took the Gerber MK11 combat knife. It was a fighting dagger originally produced in 1966 and designed on a Roman sword. It served its purpose in many wars, especially for the Americans. He put it in a sheath and clipped it on his belt on.

Lastly, he took a suppressor for the gun.

Putting on his overcoat and beanie, he replaced the slab, turned out the light and silently left his room.

* * *

Father Matthew watched Michael from his presbytery window across from the churchyard. He saw the man stealthily pick his way through the headstones, even though it was dark. Michael got into his van, started it up and disappeared into the night.

Father Matthew now walked back to his armchair and sat down wearily. As he reached for his tumbler of whisky, he looked once more at the photo of the police sketch of the man known as 'The Avenging Angel' on the front of *The Bristol Eye*. Staring back at him was the man he had grown to know as Michael.

Could he really be a killer?

Father Matthew always suspected that there was more to the man than met the eye. The younger man had never really spoken much about himself or his past.

Michael had been a good companion around the church and a good worker. He was also a good supper companion on many occasions. But at no time had Father Matthew seen anything other than a kind and thoughtful man who was down on his luck and a little lost.

Father Matthew was in turmoil.

What should he do?

He could easily phone the police now and they would be here waiting for Michael when he returned, but he decided against it.

Father Matthew decided to turn in for the night and speak with Michael himself tomorrow.

Before the priest finally got into bed, he knelt by his bedside and prayed for strength and guidance. He also prayed for Michael's soul.

* * *

Michael stood outside the block of flats at the address he had been given.

It was 1:30am and all was quiet.

He had parked well away from here.

He made his way over to the stairs and easily climbed them to the fifth floor. He began walking along the balcony to number 54.

Just as he approached, a man came out of the door. He didn't see Michael.

The man was mid-forties, Asian with a jet-black beard and hair.

He shouted back into the hallway.

"I have another bottle of vodka in the boot of my car. I won't be a minute."

He shut the door and turned around. Michael blended into the shadows of a recess and watched.

The man strolled past and went down the stairs.

Michael looked down over the balcony and saw the lights blink on a Volkswagen Golf as the man pressed the key fob to open it. He reached into the boot and produced a bottle, which he put inside his coat, and began to make his way back.

Michael returned to the recess of the wall, unclipped the Gerber and slipped it into his left palm. It felt comfortable.

Soon, he heard the man's footsteps on the stairs getting closer. They were coming along the balcony.

As the man passed Michael, he stepped out of the recess and pulled him backwards, pushing the blade of the Gerber onto his throat. Michael then whispered into the man's ear.

"Answer me this question and I might just let you live."

He felt the initial resistance drain from the man's body. The vodka bottle dropped to the floor and smashed. Instantly, the alcohol fumes rose and filled Michael's nostrils.

A sudden image sprung into his head of him, young Joe Eccles and many of Team Wolf drinking vodka in a bar somewhere in the world, but he couldn't recall where. His memories were clouded and sketchy. As quickly as the image came into his mind, it faded out again.

A voice inside his head told him to focus on the task.

"Is Muhammad Jarwar in the flat you came out of?"

The man remained silent.

Michael pushed the blade into the man's throat, drawing blood.

"I am not fucking around here. Tell me what I need to know."

The man nodded his head.

"Yes, he is in there."

"How many others?"

"Four," came the reply.

"That include you?"

"Yes," replied the man.

"How many girls?"

The man hesitated and Michael pushed harder with the blade. He let out a small whimper of fear.

"Just the one."

Michael felt his blood boil.

One young girl alone with four foul and disgusting pigs. He swallowed down his anger.

"Right, walk to the door. Do you have a key?"

The man nodded.

"Slowly get it out."

Michael walked the man to the door and got him to insert the key in the lock and open it. As he did, the man tried to break free and shout a warning, but Michael had already anticipated this and drew the blade across his windpipe slicing it open.

He then clamped his hand over the man's mouth, drove the dagger into his kidney and pulled him inside and shut the door. He now let the man drop to the carpet.

Michael cleaned his knife on the man's jacket and returned it to its sheath. He then reached inside his coat, pulled out the Glock and racked it. He screwed on the suppressor.

Moving to the left, he saw a closed door. From behind it came the sound of music and men's voices laughing.

Michael prepared himself.

He kicked the door in, burst into the room and scanned it.

On the sofa to the left was a naked girl, no more than 14 years old. A man was having intercourse with her while another was making her perform oral sex on him. A third man that he recognised as Jarwar was sat in an armchair naked watching the scene sniffing coke from a tray.

He tried to get up, but Michael was on him. He struck the man with a bullet in the centre of his chest. He slumped back into the chair.

Michael walked up to Jarwar and looked at him with disdain.

"I'm here for your soul, motherfucker."

He put a bullet through his balls and one between his eyes.

Michael now turned to the two men who had jumped up and stood with their hands raised.

"Please don't hurt us. Please," said the older of the two who had been having intercourse with the girl.

Michael looked at the girl.

He picked a throw up from an armchair and threw it to her.

"Cover yourself and leave the room."

The girl wrapped the throw around herself.

"I'm not leaving until I see these two pay for all they've done to me and my friends."

Michael saw the defiance in her eyes. He didn't argue.

He turned back to the men. They both looked pathetic, standing naked with their now flaccid penises. Both of them must have been in their fifties.

God in heaven, the girl was a child.

They started to plead.

"Please have mercy on us."

Michael levelled the gun at their heads.

"Mercy? Mercy? Where was the fucking mercy to these innocent girls? Fuck you, both."

With that, Michael put a bullet in each of their heads and two more apiece in their chests.

He turned to the girl.

"What's your name?"

"Sonia."

"Sonia, I'm Michael and these men can no longer hurt you or your friends. Now, put your clothes on. I'll drop you to the hospital where you can be looked after."

The girl broke into tears and clutched Michael.

"Thank you. Thank you."

Michael gently touched her hair.

"We have to go."

With that, they walked out of the room, stepped over the body in the hall and left.

Fifteen minutes later, Michael dropped Sonia off at A&E.

"Who are you and how did you know I was in that flat?" asked Sonia.

"Better you don't know. Now, go! It's over!"

Sonia got out of the van and looked back at Michael.

"What do I say when the police get involved?"

Michael smiled sadly.

"Tell them your guardian angel was looking out for you."

* * *

Michael waited until the girl had walked in through the sliding doors of the hospital.

He then pulled out the burner phone and dialled the one number he had in it. After two rings, it was answered.

"It's done," said Michael and cut the call.

He now knew that his time in Bristol was limited.

The police would be closing in on him very soon.

Chapter 18

Next morning, the briefing room was buzzing. Word had just filtered through of four men found dead in a flat in the riverwalk area of the city.

The room fell silent as DCI Harry Bowe walked in. His face looked grim.

He made his way to the front. When he was sure he had everybody's attention, he spoke.

"News has just come through that the bodies of four men were found dead by a cleaner in a flat in the riverwalk complex. They have all been identified as part of the grooming gang targeting young girls. Muhammad Jarwar, the ringleader, is one of the dead."

"Our boy again?" asked DS Leech.

Harry looked towards his old colleague.

"Too early to be 100% sure, but it all points to him."

"Stabbings?" queried DS Carrie French.

"One killed with a knife; the others shot execution style," answered Bowe.

"So, he isn't some looney tune. This guy is a pro," commented DS Rose.

Harry nodded.

"I think we all knew this deep down. Again, he's targeted a group we've gone after more than once and failed to get a conviction."

"If you ask me, the scum got what they deserved," said Leech.

Harry shot him an angry glare.

"Jim, don't you utter anything like that outside these four walls. Yes, all the victims were scum, but we have a police system for a reason. If everybody took the law into their own hands, there would be chaos. Plus, we'd all be out of a job."

Leech looked suitably chastised.

Harry continued.

"Yes, we have a vigilante on the loose and we can no longer deny it. Once the latest murders hit the newspapers and media, then everybody will know this as fact."

"Are we still no closer to identifying this person?" asked DC Sharma.

"I'm just about to come to that. We have had a major breakthrough on this and we now believe we know this man's identity."

Murmuring went around the room. You could cut the atmosphere with a knife.

"I'll let DS Khan take it from here as it was his hard work that found this evidence."

Khan couldn't keep the smile from his face as he took front and centre of the room.

He told the team about the visit to the Vault Gym and their discovery of the cleaner Michael. He then spoke about the contents of the locker and how DNA was obtained from a drinking bottle. Khan then revealed the identity of 'The Avenging Angel' and the latest update on him.

"The DNA belongs to a Michael Lange, known as Mick. He is ex-Forces. A captain in the SAS no less. Discharged on medical grounds from the army after his last tour in Afghanistan. He led a team on an attack on the Taliban, but they were ambushed. All Lange's men were killed and Lange received life-threatening injuries. He was the only survivor. Somehow, he made it to safety and was flown to Camp Bastion for hospital treatment to bullet and shrapnel wounds. During the operation, his heart stopped and he was technically dead for two minutes, but they got him back. Bullet wounds were dealt with and the shrapnel was removed from his left leg. But listen up, it has left him with a slight limp."

You could hear a pin drop in the room. DS Khan had their full attention.

"The injuries put pay to his career in one respect, but it was the trauma of the incident he had been involved him that scarred Lange big time. PTSD was the other cause of the discharge. He was not a well man. He had medical treatment for a short while, but then seemed to drop off the radar.

Nobody knew where he went. He went off the grid for months. Then, he suddenly reappeared in London. Outside a nightclub, he saw a pregnant woman being assaulted by a man. Lange intervened and the man pulled a blade on him. Lange fended off the knife, but then strangled the man to death. He got ten years for manslaughter, but served five.

Lange did his time with no further incident and was let out of prison around four months ago. Again, he disappeared, but eventually we believe he has turned up in Bristol, incidentally where he was born. We've looked for next of kin, but there's nobody here in Bristol. But we believe he's come back to his hometown for a reason."

Harry took over.

"Thank you, Ali."

He regarded his team.

"Our priority now is to find the Father Matthew who signed that Bible for him."

"It might be years old and he just carries it around with him…" commented DC Bailey.

"That is a possibility, but remember Duane Rawlings telling us the killer's coat smelt of incense? That's not coincidence. Either he's visiting a priest or staying with one. So, let's get on it everybody. Let's start digging and see what we can find."

Harry's phone suddenly pinged. He looked at the screen and saw that it was Superintendent Bradley.

"Right, let's get to it and keep me posted if you come up with anything. I'm required upstairs.

* * *

"What I don't understand about all of this is where is this man getting information about his targets? I know I asked you before, Harry, but I'm going to ask you again. Is there a possibility of a leak within your team?"

Harry was sat in Superintendent Bradley's office and his boss was more than agitated. He had just finished a phone call with Police Commissioner Quentin Harper. If Harper got on the phone, you could bet it was serious.

The Commissioner had told Bradley that he himself had just got off the phone with Mayor Ivan Barnes, who was far from happy about the latest developments and was demanding results.

As the old saying goes, 'shit rolls downhill'. Now, it was rolling towards Harry.

"As I told you before, sir, absolutely not. My team are watertight."

"How can you be sure, Harry? How well do you know them all? Can they be trusted?"

Harry regarded Bradley. He was angry that his team's integrity was being questioned again.

"With respect, sir, I have 20 plus years of experience, 15 of those in homicide. I have headed many a team and I would put up this one with the best. I stake my reputation on it."

"Let's hope it doesn't come to that."

Bradley then changed tack.

"This Lange character, are you sure it's him?"

"Everything points that way. We're now trying to track down the priest. When we do, I believe it will bring us to our killer."

Bradley sat back in his chair.

Harry thought that the man looked tired.

This case was taking its toll on all involved in it.

"Sir, I know the situation isn't ideal and that you're getting heat from the very top, but I promise you that we're doing everything possible to find this man. We're working 24/7 around the clock."

Bradley nodded and then allowed himself a small smile.

"I suppose you're going to be hitting me for more overtime?"

Harry returned the smile.

"Fucking right I am, sir."

* * *

Charlie Rawlings visited his son Duane who was on remand in Stonehouse Prison near Bath some 12 miles from Bristol. He had been denied bail as he was considered a flight risk.

Mr Singh was still clinging to life, but it didn't look good.

Charlie regarded his son, who looked pale and withdrawn. His usual cocky swagger was missing.

The reality of prison can be harsh. Even harsher if you go down for murder.

"We're appealing for bail again, son. Trying to get them to tag you so they know you won't try to do a runner. McGinn will do everything he can to see you don't go down as an accessory. Just hang in there. Remember, you're a Rawlings. Don't let the bastards grind you down."

Duane found a weak smile.

"Okay. Dad. I'll do my best."

Charlie reached across the table and lay a huge hand on his son's shoulder.

"Good lad."

He then changed the subject and told Duane about the latest developments.

"The fucker was right under our noses all the time working at the gym."

"Do you think he's still in Bristol or has this scared him off?" asked Duane.

"Well, this morning on the radio, I heard four Asian kiddy fiddlers were murdered last night over at the riverwalk flats. Stabbed and shot. So, I believe he's still here."

"Get him, Dad. Get this bastard and do him in. He's fucked me right up."

"You can bet on that, son."

Charlie now leant in close.

"This Bible I told you the cops found. It was signed inside by a Father Matthew. Now that name rings a bell with me. Why is that? I'm not a fucking churchgoer, so why does the name sound familiar?"

Duane thought for a moment. Then, his eyes lit up.

"Remember when I was a kid and went to that youth club for problem children. I was in the football team. I must have been about twelve then."

"Yes, I remember. You wanted to be the new Ronaldo…"

Duane laughed.

"Yeah. What the fuck happened to that idea?"

"So, what about the club?" asked Charlie.

"It was run by a priest. His name was Father Matthew Munroe. Remember?"

"Shit, yes. That was over at The Sacred Heart parish. Do you think he's still there? That was a good six years ago."

"Got to be worth checking, don't you think?"

Charlie slapped his hand on his son's shoulder yet again.

"Well done, son. I think we're onto something."

Charlie stood up.

"I'll be back soon. Keep strong and thanks again."

When Charlie got outside and into his car, he rang Leroy Curtis.

"Meet me at the gym. I have a lead."

Chapter 19

Harry was back in his office after the meeting with Superintendent Bradley. Christmas was now only days away and he longed for a few days holiday, but deep down, he knew that if this killer wasn't caught soon, there would be very little festive celebrations.

He knew Carol had some hospital leave and would be off for Christmas Day and Boxing Day. He hoped they could spend that time together.

They had both been busy of late and hadn't spent much quality time together. He was aware of this fact.

The other night when he had got home late, Carol was already in bed. As he heated up a meal that had been left for him, he noticed half a dozen holiday brochures supposedly left casually on the kitchen table. He knew that it was his wife's subtle way of suggesting that it was about time they had a holiday.

Harry had picked the top one up. It was called *Winter Sun Breaks*. As his meal warmed, he flicked through it. All the places certainly looked inviting. With the icy blast of weather that the UK had recently been experiencing, the images of sunkissed beaches looked idyllic.

Now sat at his desk, he made a mental note to talk about a holiday away with Carol later.

Suddenly, his phone rang.

Harry picked it up to see the caller ID said Jim Leech.

"Jim, how's it going?"

"We're onto a few leads, guv. I went online and found that there is a National Register of Clergy. It lists all the ordained clergy, bishops, priests and deacons in the Church of England who are authorised to minister. I went through the data and came up with two Father Matthews in the Bristol area. DC Bailey and I are on our way to see them now."

"That's great news, Jim. Keep me posted."

When Harry put the phone down, he felt that old familiar tingle of adrenaline once again in his belly. The hunt was well and truly on and he sensed that he was closing in on his prey.

* * *

Michael had got home late after his visit to the flat. He found sleep almost impossible. When he did close his eyes, his dreams were full of horror and bloodshed. Recent memories and ones from the past morphed together into terrible nightmares.

But always within these nightmares was the face of young Joe Eccles. One minute, he was smiling, drinking vodka and dancing; the next, his legless body was crawling across the floor, pleading for Michael to help him. Then, his head exploded as the bullets hit him.

As dawn broke, Michael pulled his exhausted body from his bed and boiled the kettle, desperate for a coffee. He regarded his haggard features in a mirror that sat on the window ledge.

Going to his kit bag, he found a razor, shaving foam and scissors. Back in front of the mirror, he began to shave off his beard and tidy his hair. Clean features may buy him a bit more time.

He had seen his face on the front of the tabloids. He knew that his time was ticking down here in Bristol. For now, his work was finished. He contemplated returning to Spain and lying low for a while until the calling came once more.

The names of the souls he had been given had now been delivered. He had repaid his dues.

Before he left, he needed to talk to Father Matthew. The man had been so kind to him. He couldn't just go without saying goodbye.

* * *

Michael found Father Matthew standing in the graveyard sipping on a mug of coffee. The man was deep in thought. He coughed to make his presence known and the priest seemed to come out of his reverie.

"Good morning, Michael. I didn't hear you there."

"Morning, Father."

"You look different, Michael," said the priest, surveying him.

"Time for a clean-up and change of image. I've let myself go of late."

"It suits you."

Father Matthew looked back to the graves that he had been studying.

"So many people buried here. Some of these graves are over 100 years old, some older. I often wonder does heaven ever get full? Is there a limit on the number of people that can actually get in there? Imagine turning up at the pearly gates and St Peter turning you away saying, 'Come back in a week's time'."

Father Matthew laughed at his little joke.

"I suppose you could say the same about hell," replied Michael, "There are many evil people on this planet. Maybe their souls have also got to wait."

Father Matthew regarded the younger man.

"That's a good point. I often ask myself is heaven fuller than hell or vice versa?"

"God can only truly decide who goes to heaven," answered Michael.

"What a job. What a responsibility," said Father Matthew.

"It is, Father, but remember, he has helpers. He is not alone."

"True enough."

There was a moment of silence. Then, Father Matthew asked.

"Will you come to supper this evening at 8:00pm?"

For a moment, Michael hesitated, but then he spoke.

"I will, Father, but it will be my last supper as I am moving on soon."

"As you wish, my son. I will miss you."

"Father, can I ask... I haven't been much of a churchgoer in my time, but I was baptised a Catholic. Can I take confession before supper tonight?"

Father Matthew nodded.

"Yes, you may. Let's meet inside the church at 7:00pm."

Michael looked at the older man.

"Can I ask that you wait to hear my confession before you do anything?"

It was now the priest's turn to look puzzled.

"Do anything?"

Michael smiled.

"I saw the newspaper in the church porch. You must have forgotten and left it there. I expect you have put two and two together by now."

Michael saw the concern on the man's face.

"Don't worry, Father. You're in no danger from me."

Father Matthew smiled faintly.

"In that case, you have my promise. I will see you tonight."

* * *

Later in the day, Harry received another call from DS Leech. Leech informed him that he had tracked down the two clergymen.

One was at St Mary's in a part of Bristol called Clifton and the other was at Holy Cross in another part of the city known as St Anne's. Both had read about the murders, but neither of them knew the man in the sketch.

Leech had shown them the Bible and inscription, but again, they had never seen it before. It was a dead end.

Maybe, as suggested earlier, the Bible was given to this Michael by a priest from another city or town. Maybe even another country.

Harry had cursed. He was sure that they could have tracked down the priest. Maybe he had got it all wrong.

He dreaded the phone call that he would have to make to Bradley. He decided to leave it until tomorrow.

Harry made it home for an early dinner.

"Well, this is an unexpected surprise, DCI. Bowe," said Carol as Harry walked into the kitchen.

"I thought I might catch you with the milkman," joked Harry.

Carol laughed.

"That was this morning, Harry. It was the plumber who just left five minutes ago."

Harry took Carol in his arms and kissed her. She was fresh out of the shower and smelt of coconut.

Harry now moved to the fridge and got himself out a bottle of Budweiser.

"Pour me a glass of white while you're there, please, love."

Carol began to chop up vegetables.

"So, how was your day?" asked Harry as he handed his wife her drink.

She momentarily stopped the chopping and took a sip of the ice cool chardonnay.

"Heaven," she sighed, "Work was the usual continuous stream of people coming through A&E. Most not meant to be there. Although we did have a nasty car accident emergency. Four people needed to be cut out of their two vehicles down on the bypass."

"How are they?" asked Harry as he took a pull on his beer bottle.

"They're all in intensive care, but stable. They were lucky."

Carol now headed over to the slow cooker on the worktop, which was simmering away with some fantastic smells emanating from it.

"Sausage casserole. It should be ready in half an hour or so."

"Great," replied Harry, "I'm just going to grab a quick shower."

* * *

Over dinner, Carol asked Harry how his day had gone. She, of course, knew all about the case he was working on. You could hardly fail not to know as coverage of it seemed to be everywhere.

Harry told her about the latest developments and the disappointment of not finding this Father Matthew.

"That's tough, Harry, but I'm thinking Jim Leech looked only at the records of clergy from the Church of England. Is that correct?"

Harry finished off the last mouthful of the delicious casserole and wiped his mouth with a napkin.

"Yes, that's about the size of it."

Carol took another sip of her wine.

"What if the priest is Catholic? Did he not look on their register?"

Harry was taking a swig of his beer when he stopped mid-swallow and lowered the bottle.

"Shit, Carol. I never thought of that. Of course. Jim never checked that out."

Harry picked his phone up from the table and speed dialled Jim Leech's number. He answered almost immediately.

"Hello, guv. Everything alright?"

"Yes, Jim. Look, sorry to disturb you, but when you're back on duty tomorrow, look up the Catholic clergy register for this Father Matthew. You only checked the Church of England one, right?"

"Christ, it never crossed my mind being C of E myself. I'll get on it first thing."

Harry cut the call and sat back in his seat smiling.

"Carol, you're a bloody diamond."

Carol smiled.

"In that case, you can wash up and make the coffee. I'm off to watch *Call the Midwife*."

Chapter 20

Earlier that day, Charlie Rawlings and Leroy Curtis had been doing some detective work of their own. Their car pulled up outside Sacred Heart Church.

Charlie instantly remembered it.

He told Leroy to stay in the car. The less the man was seen by people, the better.

He walked past the church until he spotted what used to be the parish church hall. This was where the youth club had run and where Father Matthew helped the kids. It was not only football played there, but also table tennis, cricket and even darts.

Duane had been a handful as a child, but this place had given him a bit of purpose for a while. Until he got involved in street crime.

Deep down, Charlie knew that he wasn't much in the way of a role model for his boy, but the life he led was the only one he knew. He was too old in the tooth now to change. Maybe Duane's path was already decided when he was born.

Charlie walked up to the doors and tried them. They were locked and it was dark inside. He walked back towards the church.

An elderly priest suddenly appeared from the doorway.

"Can I help you? I'm Father Healy, the parish priest."

"Hello, Father. Can I ask, is the youth club still running and does Father Matthew still run it?"

"In answer to your questions, it's no on both counts. The club shut about five years ago. Nobody was attending. Crying shame really. I blame all those video games. Kids these days don't seem to want to get off the sofa and exercise."

Charlie smiled.

"I can't argue with that. What about Father Matthew?"

"He left shortly after. He moved on to run St Mathias Church at Redly Park."

"Is he still there?" Charlie asked.

The old priest rubbed his chin thoughtfully.

"As far as I know, he is. He's done great work with the homeless in that area, I believe."

Father Healy walked down the steps towards Charlie.

"May I ask what you want him for?"

Charlie was prepared for this question.

"I was passing in the area. My son used to go to the youth club and Father Matthew was very instrumental in his future development. I just wanted to pass on my thanks to him for all his hard work."

Father Healy nodded.

"Indeed, Father Matthew did a great job here and I was sad to see him go."

"Well, thanks for your help, Father. I must be going."

As Charlie walked off, the old priest called out to him.

"If you do catch up with Father Matthew at St Mathias, please give him my regards."

Charlie glanced back at the old man.

"I will certainly do that, Father. I'm looking forward to seeing him again myself."

* * *

Charlie got back into the car.

"Any luck?" asked Leroy.

"Apparently, he's at St Mathias Church, which is coincidentally close to the Patels' shop. I think we're on to something. According to the old priest I just spoke with, our Father Matthew likes helping out the homeless and waifs and strays."

"Do we go there now?" asked Leroy.

"No. We'll go there this evening under the cover of darkness. If this man is holing up there, we need to make sure we're not seen. Understand?"

"Perfectly, Charlie. If this geezer is there, I'll take him out. No sweat."

Charlie looked at Leroy Curtis and smiled.

"That's exactly why I contacted you. You may have to take the priest out as well if he causes us problems. Are you okay with that?"

Now it was Leroy's time to smile.

"Any chance of me going through the pearly gates is long gone. I can feel the fires of hell burning my ass as I speak."

Charlie laughed as he pulled away from the curb and headed home.

* * *

"Bless me, Father, for I have sinned. It's a very long time since my last confession."

Michael was in the confessional box of St Mathias Church.

Father Matthew was in the box opposite to take the confession.

"Okay, Michael. In your own time,' said Father Matthew.

There were a few moments of silence and then Michael spoke.

"As you may have already guessed, Father, I am the killer that has been on the front of all the newspapers. I had to clear the streets of all the filth. Nobody else was going to do it and criminals are just allowed to walk freely taunting the police who are powerless to do anything."

"You know killing is a sin?" said Father Matthew.

"If you follow the Ten Commandments, yes, but I never have," replied Michael, "I've spent the best part of my life in the army. I was a Captain in the SAS. I was Captain Mick Lange. I killed many men in the name of war. I also killed woman and children for the same cause. I grew to like it. I was good at it. So good I craved the killing like a junkie craves their next fix.

My parents were staunch Catholics. They brought me up in the faith. I believe my father wanted me to take holy orders and become a priest like yourself, but that was never going to be. My calling came early, but not for the priesthood; it was for the military. It didn't sit well with my parents, but there was no going back. I was born to be a soldier."

"So, what went wrong? Why are you no longer in the army?"

Michael told the story of the failed mission and the wiping out of his team. He told of the horrors he had seen and how he had found his way to safety badly wounded and how eventually he was medically discharged from the army.

Father Matthew listened in silence.

"On the operating table, I died for two minutes, but in those two minutes, I went to heaven. I am convinced of this. Why not hell you might ask? I've asked myself the same thing many times.

God spoke to me. He told me I wasn't ready to die. He told me to go back. He needed a man like me to fight for him and his cause on earth. He spoke of how a great percentage of humanity has disappointed him with their behaviour and their lack of love and respect for their fellow man. They needed to be punished, just as his son Jesus cleansed the temple by throwing out the undesirables, telling them that this is a house of God, not a den of thieves.

God then told me I was no longer Mick Lange, but now Michael the Archangel and that Michael is the protector of the people and the church. He leads the army of God and escorts people into the afterlife. This is what I have done."

Father Matthew was stunned by Michael's words.

This man truly believed that he had spoken to God and he had instructed him to send his wrath down to the sinners.

"Why tell me this now, Michael?"

"Because my work is done here for now."

"How do you know this? Has God told you?"

"God, as you know, Father, works in mysterious ways. He has many other disciples working for him on earth of the same mind as me. I managed to contact one such person who instructed me who God wanted punished."

"Maybe you have his message wrong. Maybe he wanted you to share your experiences of war, bloodshed and violence. Maybe he wanted you to tell people that is not the way forward," said the priest.

Michael smiled.

"Don't be so naïve, Father. There will always be a need for soldiers. Wasn't it George Orwell who said, 'People sleep peaceably in their beds at night because rough men stand ready to do violence on their behalf'."

Father Matthew countered the statement.

"Didn't Robert K. Ressler, former head of the FBI say once, 'Whoever fights monsters should see to it that in the process he does not become a monster. And when you look into an abyss, the abyss also looks into you'?"

"I don't see myself as a monster, Father. Rather, I see myself as a crusader."

"So, are you asking me for forgiveness?" asked Father Matthew.

"No. I do not seek or need forgiveness. The killings were done in God's name."

Father Matthew shook his head in the darkness of the confessional.

"Michael, isn't that half the reason the world is at war with each other because they hide their crimes behind the word of the Lord? How are you any different to the warlords, dictators and terrorists out there?"

There was a long silence. Then, Michael spoke. His voice was raised.

"I don't have all the answers. When I meet God again, I will ask him. I will ask him why it took so much pain and suffering in this world before he acted. Why has he let rapists, paedophiles and serial killers get away with the terrible things they have done?

The people I killed were scum that deserved to die. I have done society a favour getting rid of them. They can never hurt anybody ever again. Surely, you can see that."

"Why are you telling me all this if you don't seek absolution?" asked Father Matthew.

"The reason I spoke to you in the confessional is I know that nothing said in here can be repeated outside the walls of this box. Am I right?"

"You know you are right, Michael."

Michael continued.

"I owed you an explanation because you have been so good to me. The police will be coming sooner or later. I need time to get away. I know they will question you and, without the sanctity of the confessional box, your faith would have obliged you to tell the truth."

"Very clever, Michael. Of course, what you say is true. So, now what?"

"Will you break bread with me one more time? Can we dine together? By the morning, I'll be gone."

Father Matthew blessed himself.

"I can't condone what you've done, Michael, but I believe your motives were genuine. Yes, we will break bread one more time."

A minute later, Father Matthew heard Michael's confessional door open, followed by footsteps walking away.

Michael called back.

"I will see you over at your house Father for 8:00pm. I am going to wash and change and pack my belongings.

* * *

Outside the church, the black BMW silently pulled up on the grass verge, avoiding the gravel driveway.

Inside the car, Charlie Rawlings and Leroy Curtis checked their firearms.

"There are lights on in the church, so let's try there first."

Both men got out of the car and were careful when shutting the doors. Using the grass, they walked as far as they could on it until they stepped off onto the porchway.

Charlie went up to the impressive oak door and turned the wrought iron handle.

The door opened.

Charlie looked at Leroy.

"Ready?"

The large, black man was a figure of pure focus as he nodded.

Chapter 21

When Michael had left, Father Matthew sat in the quiet of the confessional box. What he had just heard was quite amazing. Could this man have actually entered the doorway of heaven and spoke to God?

Father Matthew had devoted his life to Christ, but even he questioned the existence of a higher being in his darkest moments.

He totally believed in the existence of Jesus the man, but he had to admit that sometimes he struggled with God the superpower.

Michael had sounded so convinced, but he must have also been on all sorts of medications for his injuries. Maybe it had all been in his mind. He had gone through terrible trauma and it was a well-documented fact that people suffering extreme trauma could manufacture and imagine all sorts.

The death of the young soldier in his care had greatly affected Michael. Maybe some sort of guilt had driven him on to do what he had done. A sense of trying to do something positive because he felt that he had let his team, and especially the boy, down.

Father Matthew heard the church door open. It was late for visitors on a cold, dark December evening. He opened up the door of the confessional box and looked across the bank of pews. He saw two men standing there.

Although he didn't want to appear judgemental, he had to conclude that they didn't look like the sort of men who you would find in a church. From his days as an army chaplain, he recognised these men as being potentially dangerous.

"Can I help you, gentlemen? I'm just about to shut up shop, so to speak."

"Are you Father Matthew Monroe?"

"Why yes, I am. What may I do for you?"

In a flash, both men levelled their guns on the priest.

"Where is he, Father?" asked Charlie.

"Dear Lord, how dare you draw a gun in the sanctity of God's house?"

"Spare me the lecture, Father. Now, where is he?"

"Who? I don't know what you're talking about."

Rawlings shook his head.

"Father, you talk about us ruining the sanctity of the church, yet you, a priest, stand there and lie in it. So, I will ask you once more. Where is this nutcase that calls himself Michael? I know you've given him shelter here."

"You must have the wrong person. There is nobody here of that name."

Rawlings nodded to Curtis.

The big man moved like a panther and grabbed the priest.

From his pocket, Curtis pulled out a stun gun and pressed the button. A crackle of blue light flashed across the top. He then pressed it into Father Matthew's chest. The man howled in pain and fell onto the cold stone floor.

Rawlings loomed over the stricken priest.

"My friend here is a man of very few words. He will hurt you badly if you don't give up this lunatic. How in God's name can you protect such a person?"

Father Matthew rolled over on his back and looked at his attackers.

"I don't know what you're talking about."

Curtis moved in with the stun gun again, holding it on the priest longer than before. This time, the man screamed out in agony.

"Either you're a very brave man or a fool, Father. But the reality of the situation is if you truly believe in God, you are very close to meeting him."

Father Matthew could hardly hear the man's voice through the excruciating pain that wracked his whole body.

* * *

As Michael came out of his room and climbed the stairs to the church, he heard the bloodcurdling scream. He slowed his pace and cautiously ascended the remaining steps.

He quietly opened the door at the top and peaked into the church. He immediately saw two large figures looming over the fallen body of Father Matthew. Both held guns and the bigger of the two held something else.

Suddenly, whatever the man held in his hand crackled. Michael knew instantly that it was a stun gun. He didn't know who they were, but he quickly surmised two things.

Firstly, they were here for him. And secondly, they didn't look like police.

His instincts were to rush out to save his friend, but he knew that would be suicide. So, he silently pulled the door up and descended the stairs to his room.

Once inside, he opened a large holdall that he had packed and fished inside for his weapons. He pulled out the Browning and checked the clip. He then fished out the tanto.

Michael now shrugged on his coat and pulled on his hat and gloves. He exited the room and once more climbed the stairs.

* * *

"Father, one more shot from this stun gun and it'll be over for you. You've shown you are a tough man, but as the saying goes, 'the graveyard is full of heroes'." said Rawlings.

Father Matthew was in a bad way, but he gritted his teeth and responded.

"Well, if you kill me, you'll never find Michael, will you?"

Rawlings smiled.

"So, he is here. Tell me where!"

"Go to hell!" hissed Father Matthew.

Curtis leant forward again and administered the stun gun.

This time, the priest lapsed into unconsciousness.

"Is he dead?" asked Rawlings.

Curtis checked the carotid pulse in the man's neck.

"He has a faint pulse, but I don't know how strong his heart is."

Just then, a voice spoke.

"Leave the priest alone and step away from him now."

Both men turned to see a man clad from head to toe in black, pointing a pistol at them.

"Lose the guns. Slowly place them on the ground and step away from the altar."

Both men did as they had been told.

"So, you're this Michael character who has gone on a killing spree?" stated Rawlings.

"That's right," replied Michael.

"You're also the man who dished out a hiding to my son and his mates in the Patels' corner shop?"

Michael frowned for a moment and then a flicker of recognition came to his eyes.

"Ah, the bunch of little shits who tried to rob the shop and stabbed the old man. I remember. You are lucky I spared their miserable lives, but they weren't on my agenda."

"Do you know who I am?" said Rawlings incredulously.

"No. Should I?"

"My name is Charlie Rawlings and I run this side of Bristol. This is my manor. I have kept control of it as I see fit for ten years and then you waltz in and reenact a bad day in Bosnia. Who the fuck are you? Did the Albanians send you to test me out? To see if I was who I said I was?"

"I know nothing of what you're talking about. I am God's messenger. Michael the Archangel. I am here to deliver the souls of the evil."

Rawlings looked at Curtis.

"Do you hear this fruitcake? He must have escaped from a fucking loony bin."

Michael walked forward.

"Enough talk. You've come here looking for me and now you've found me."

Michael looked down at the silent figure of Father Matthew.

"But you've hurt a good man and you'll pay for that. Now, turn around and face the altar."

Both men slowly did what they were told.

"Now drop to your knees."

The men hesitated.

Michael walked closer and pushed his gun alternately into the back of their heads.

"Get down!"

This time, both men complied.

"Now pray for your souls."

A voice behind Michael momentarily caught his attention.

"Don't, Michael. I beg you in the name of God. Enough killing."

Michael looked back to see Father Matthew trying to pull himself up onto a bench.

In that split second, Leroy Curtis reacted. He spun around and lunged forward, tackling Michael around the legs.

Michael fell back from the force and smashed his head on one of the pews. His gun fell from his hand.

The big man was straight on top of him and dropped a headbutt into Michael's face. It was followed by two huge punches. Curtis picked Michael up from the floor like a rag doll in a crushing bear hug and spoke.

"I'm going to squeeze your fucking lungs out through your mouth, you motherfucker."

Michael was bleeding and badly stunned, but he still had that steely resolve. As he was lifted up in the air, he slapped both of his palms over the big man's ears.

Curtis howled in shock and pain.

Michael then stuck a pair of hooking punches into the temples, the thinnest part of the skull an inch back from the eyes.

The big man's grip loosened.

Michael now smashed a headbutt down onto the bridge of Curtis's nose. The grip released and he was dropped to the floor as the big, black man was momentarily incapacitated.

Rawlings now ran forward and swung a punch at Michael's head, but Michael speared him with a front lunge kick right in the solar plexus, sending him crashing backwards into a large display of flowers.

Curtis stumbled forward again and grabbed for Michael's neck, but he had unclipped the tanto dagger by now and had it in his hand.

Michael drove it into the big man's torso and ripped up and down before extracting it. Leroy Curtis came to a halt and looked down at his protruding entrails. He frantically tried to push them back in, but it was in vain.

He sank to his knees and looked at Michael. A small grin played on his face as if he knew that he had been beaten by a better man. Michael closed in and drove the dagger into his right eye, penetrating the brain. The big man toppled forward to the ground.

Michael now switched his attention to where Rawlings had fallen, but he was not there. He spun around and scanned the church, but there was no sign of him.

Going to the far side of the church, Michael hit all the light switches, bathing the whole place in brightness.

Michael found and retrieved his gun, but also noticed that one of the two guns that the men had put down were missing.

He cautiously moved amongst the pews, expecting Rawlings to pounce out on him at any moment.

The seating area was empty.

A cursory search of the confessional boxes revealed nothing either.

The man had gone.

Michael now focused his attention on Father Matthew, who was sat on the end of a bench. He was in a bad way.

"Hang in there, Father, and I'll get you some help."

Michael produced his burner phone and dialled 999.

He asked for emergency services to hurry up and come to St Mathias church, telling them that Father Matthew had suffered a suspected heart attack. He hoped that this would get the paramedics there quicker. They wanted him to stay on the line and give them his details, but he cut the call.

Michael looked at his friend.

"The paramedics are on their way. I am sorry for all the pain I've caused you. Can you ever forgive me?"

Father Matthew said nothing, then slipped back into unconsciousness.

Chapter 22

DCI Harry Bowe was driving into work at 7:30am when he got a call from DS Rose. Before he even took it on his Bluetooth, he had a bad feeling in his stomach.

"Yes, Diane. What have you got?"

"Another murder, sir."

"Who is it this time?"

"The man had no identity on him. The coroner has taken him away and is going to run fingerprints and dental records," said DS Rose.

"How did he die?"

"Knife wounds again."

Harry was silent.

"Sir, here's the interesting thing."

"He was killed in St Mathias Church and the priest of this church is a Father Matthew Monroe."

Harry's ears pricked up at the name.

"Is this our priest?"

"I believe it is, but he has been rushed to hospital. He's in a bad way. It looks like he was tortured using a stun gun."

"Shit. Did the dead guy do this?"

"We found a stun gun in his jacket pocket, so I presume, yes. By the look of the crime scene, some sort of fight ensued before this man died. The dead man was built like an NFL linebacker, but again, it didn't deter our boy."

"No sign of him in or around the church?" asked Harry.

"No, sir, but below the church in the crypt, we found a room kitted out with a bed, sink and toilet. It looks like somebody has recently been staying here. The SOCO guys are giving it the once over. For now, the church is sealed off as a crime scene."

"Okay, Diane. Who have you got with you?"

"DC Bailey and DC Sharma."

"Right, all of you stay put for now in case anything turns up. What hospital did the priest go to?"

"He was taken to Southfields, sir."

Harry knew it well. It was the hospital where his wife Carol worked and she was probably there now starting her shift.

"I put DC Stewart on Father Matthew's door just in case," said Rose.

"Good thinking. I'm heading over there to see if the priest is well enough to talk. Inform the team about the latest developments, please and ask DS Leech, when he checks the Catholic clergy register, to let us know if there is only one Father Matthew on it."

"Will do, sir."

Harry rang off.

The chase was on again.

* * *

When Harry got to the hospital, he went straight to the desk and flashed his badge. He asked what ward Father Matthew was on and the room number.

The nurse on duty told him that it was Ward 6, room number 10. She told him that the man was still very poorly. He was conscious and could speak, but Harry was not to tire him.

Harry got in the lift and found his way to Ward 6. He walked along the corridor and soon saw DC Stewart sat on a plastic chair outside room 10 fiddling with his phone.

He suddenly saw his DCI approaching and hurriedly pocketed the phone and stood up.

"It's okay, Stewart. Relax. No need to shit yourself. Sit back down," said Harry.

Stewart's face reddened slightly as he returned to his chair.

"All quiet?" asked Harry.

"Yes, guv," said the younger man, "I've been here from late last night when he was brought in."

Harry nodded.

"Right, go get some breakfast in the canteen. I'll be here for a little while."

PC Stewart's face brightened.

"Thank you, guv."

Harry knocked on the door and went in.

He surveyed the man propped up on pillows in the bed. He had a drip in his left arm and was connected to a bleeping machine. Harry wasn't a great lover of hospitals, even though he had visited dozens in his career. He was fortunate that he never had to be in one since he had his appendix out when he was 14 years old.

The priest appeared to be sleeping, but as Harry drew closer to the bed, the man opened his eyes. Harry introduced himself and showed his badge.

"How are you feeling?"

The man shifted uncomfortably in the bed.

"Like my whole insides have been fried."

Harry smiled.

"I promise I won't be here too long. Just a few questions."

The priest nodded wearily.

"What happened last night?"

Father Matthew told the full story from the time the two men entered the church to Michael killing the big, black guy.

Harry listened without interruption. He jotted down notes as the man spoke.

"Who were these men?"

"When I was semi-conscious, I recall one of them told Michael that he was Charlie Rawlings. I thought I recognised his face. His boy used to play football at a youth club I ran some years back. Last night, he mentioned something to Michael about him beating his son up."

This made sense to Harry. The pieces were beginning to come together.

"This must have been the incident in the Patels' shop recently. This Michael, have you been sheltering him?"

The priest nodded.

"Yes, I look after homeless or lost souls when I can. This man just walked into my church. I felt sorry for him. He looked down on his luck. I took him in and offered him shelter and a handyman's job around the place."

"Did you realise eventually that this man was the killer we were looking for?"

"Yes. When I saw the drawing on the front page of the newspaper."

"Did you confront him about it?"

"Yes, I did."

Harry leant forward in his chair.

"What did he say?"

The priest broke into a fit of coughing.

Harry poured some water from a jug at the bedside into a glass and offered it to him. Father Matthew took it and had a few sips. The coughing ceased.

"He confessed in the confessional box. What he said was between him and I and God, of course."

Harry smiled ruefully.

"So, you're not going to tell me then?"

Father Matthew looked at the policeman.

"Ordinarily, that would be correct. But on this occasion, although Michael confessed to me, he didn't seek absolution and neither did he see that he had done wrong. So, in that case, I will not be breaking the sanctity of the confessional box."

Harry sat back in his chair.

"Tell me everything, Father."

* * *

When Harry left the hospital, he now had a clearer picture about the man called Michael, or Mick Lange, ex-soldier.

From what the priest had told him, the man thought that he was on a mission for God. Killing and then delivering souls for judgement. He was convinced that he was Michael the Archangel, God's most powerful and trusted ally.

Something had happened to Lange when he was in the SAS, something so traumatic that it made him truly believe that he was the avenging angel, doing God's bidding and ridding the world of evil using his considerable military expertise.

Another war machine gone AWOL. A loose cannon that was forgotten by those who should have helped the man.

Part of Harry felt empathy for him, but he now knew that he must bring the killing to an end.

Harry pulled into a garage for petrol and also decided to grab a takeaway coffee. As he waited in line to pay, he picked up the latest copy of *The Bristol Eye*. He read the front-page news stemming from the press conference. Goodie was weaving his writing magic and loving every minute of it.

Harry put the paper down as he paid. When he got back to his car and drove off, something niggled him about the piece he had just read in the paper. It then came to him.

The article had given a full description of this Michael, which was standard knowledge, but Goodie had also mentioned that he walked with a limp on his left leg. That information was only privy to him and his team.

How did Goodie know?

Had Bradley been right all along and there was a leak in his team?

Before he could even consider that possibility, he first needed to talk to Goodie.

Chapter 23

Tommy Good received a text message at 8:00am. The message asked for a meet. The location was under the flyover bridge of the M32.

It was now 8:40am and he was at the meeting place sat in his car.

He lowered the driver's window down a bit as he puffed on his vape. The smell of pineapple and watermelon filled the car.

He was in a good mood.

He had received a call last night from the offices of *The Sun* newspaper, asking if he would be interested in a job position coming up. They had read his articles concerning what was now known as 'The Avenging Angel Murders' and they liked his style and flair for a good story. They had also seen his performance at the press conference.

Tommy had made an appointment to go up to London to meet up in between the Christmas and New Year's holidays. He was sure that he was moving onto something big. At last, he could get out of the city and say goodbye to *The Bristol Eye* once and for all. Hopefully, there would be more challenging reporting ahead for him.

He was sorry that he had fallen out with Harry Bowe, but as they say, to make an omelette you have to break a few eggs. Playing safe didn't get you anywhere. Playing safe kept you editor of a backwater rag.

Now, it was time to swim with the big fish. Big money, celebrity, glitz and glamour. Piers Morgan, I'm coming for you.

Yes, Thomas Henry Good was on the up and up at last.

Suddenly, a tap on the passenger side window startled him enough to drop his vape. He retrieved it and pressed the unlock button on the dashboard. The door opened and a man got in.

"Morning, Goodie. Thanks for meeting me."

"No worries. What is it you want?"

Michael leaned back in the seat.

"Where do I find a Charlie Rawlings?"

"Charlie Rawlings! What do you want with that nutjob?" asked Tommy.

Michael told Goodie what had happened in the church the previous night.

Goodie listened as Michael told his story. When he had finished, Tommy blew his cheeks out.

"Fucking hell, Mick. You sure live life on the edge."

"The name is Michael."

"Yeah. Okay. Michael. Obviously, you've pissed Rawlings off. His son is inside awaiting trial for possible accomplice to murder, but there is also a rumour of Rawlings doing some big business deal. Maybe you've spooked him into thinking you're trying to muscle in with these killings. Discrediting him as he likes to think he owns south Bristol."

"He sent a guy to kill me and didn't succeed," said Michael, "I owe him a visit to deliver his soul for retribution."

"Listen, Michael. We agreed the killings are over now. It's time for you to move on. The police net is closing in. DCI Bowe will not rest until he finds you, so don't make it easy for him."

"If you don't help me, Goodie, I'll find him myself. I've kept my part of the bargain and cleared the debt I owed you and also done what the Lord asked of me, but I can't let scum like Rawlings walk these streets. He does not deserve to live."

Goodie pleaded with Michael.

"You kill Rawlings and you'll start a turf war here. That can't happen. Yes, Rawlings is an evil man, but he has his finger in many pies here in Bristol and has many people in his pocket, councillors and police among them. He keeps his own law and order on the streets."

"Where does he live? Tell me, Goodie. God has instructed me to take his soul."

"Mick... I mean, Michael. For fuck's sake, God hasn't told you anything. I was the one who told you who to kill. I was the one who gave you the information, the times, the places. Not God. That is all in your head."

Michael looked confused.

"You told me God had also spoken to you and instructed you to help me with my missions."

Goodie smiled.

"I fucking lied. I lied so you would clear our streets of some of the filth that has been clogging it up and provide me with some sensational headlines. The police are powerless to stop these criminals. I am sick of reporting about evil people escaping conviction. The world is getting worse. I want to be reporting on success stories, something uplifting for the public. Christ knows, they deserve it. Hell, you went for it, Michael. Believing you're on some fucking crusade for God. The army created you and, in the end, they fucked you up and left you to your own devices."

Michael was silent.

Goodie continued.

"As for me, the only thing my reporting crusade against the criminals of this city has done is get me death threats. I was glad you were there to send out a message to the criminal fraternity that comeuppance was on the way. Since your reign of terror, crime rates on the streets have dropped and evil scum are hiding in fear. Between us, we did a good job, whatever your personal reasons."

Michael stared at Goodie.

"When I was in the SAS, I promised your sister Angela that I would look after her boy Joe. I did all I could for him, but I didn't see the ambush that killed him coming. I couldn't save him, but when I returned here to Bristol and learnt from you that Angela had taken her own life through grief, you made the guilt I felt even worse. You heard my story and then told me that God had also spoken to you. That if I did what you asked, my guilt would be swept away and I would have absolution for what happened to your nephew. You lied. You fucking used me."

"Yes, but it worked out for us both. You did do a good thing and absolved yourself by killing the scum. Your conscious can be clear. Angela would hold no malice towards you. I lost a sister and a nephew. You owed me," said Goodie, "We were friends as children and we always said, no matter where we went in life, we would look out for each other and you did that. So, please go and get on with your life. Whatever selfish motives I have, I don't want to see you in prison."

"I can't rest until I find Rawlings. It's my duty to punish him," said Michael.

Tommy Good sighed.

"Then, you're on your own. You won't hear from me again, Michael."

Michael regarded the man he had always called a friend.

In their childhood, they had been inseparable until the army came calling for Mick Lange and university and journalism called for Thomas Good.

Michael had been close to his sister Angela too and they had been an item for a brief time, but it was only a silly teenage fling that didn't last long.

When he had joined the army, he regularly wrote to Angela and Tommy and kept in touch as much as he could over the years.

Then, in one letter, Angela told him that she had found somebody and they had been going out a while. They were now engaged to be married. A man named Ronnie Eccles.

Mick was glad for her. She seemed happy. A year later, she wrote to say that she was expecting a child. Nine months on, she told Mick that she had a boy and he was named Joe. She said her and her husband Ronnie had been disowned by their parents as it had been a mixed marriage. Racial tensions and prejudice were strong back then.

Over the years, the pressure and the tension put great strain on their marriage, resulting in Ronnie walking out on Angela and then six-year-old Joe.

Tommy Good, her brother, became her rock and he supported her financially, as well as being there to help on a daily basis with Joe. Tommy became like a surrogate dad. He loved the boy like his own.

When Joe Eccles was 17, he joined the army. He was a bright lad. He became a paratrooper and, by the age of 24, he had passed selection for the SAS and finally became part of Wolf Team run by Captain Mick Lange.

Mick was over the moon when he learnt Joe Eccles had joined his team. He promised Angela and Tommy that he would take good care of him and keep an eye out while he was his Captain. Mick had grown to like the young man who was a bundle of energy and fun, but also a damned good soldier. They had experienced many exciting times together, along with the rest of Wolf Team.

They felt invincible. They feared nothing or nobody. They loved what they did, but that one fateful night changed it all forever.

Mick had often thought about it and wondered if he could have done anything different. He was well aware that they didn't need to go on that mission, but men in the SAS can't just sit around on their hands doing babysitting duties. They were warriors born to fight.

Mick knew that all those men who lost their lives that night wanted to be there. Nobody forced them. Still, the guilt of losing them, especially Joe, lay heavy on him. He also realised that he had somehow survived for a reason. God had bigger plans for him.

Eventually, when he was strong enough physically and mentally, he had contacted Tommy and told him that he was coming to Bristol to see him. It was only then that he learnt of Angela's recent death. She had jumped of the Clifton Suspension Bridge. She couldn't face life without her son. Mick was hit for six and the grief and guilt he had been feeling only got worse.

When he met up with Tommy, he had told him his side of the story, covering every detail. This was when Tommy saw an opportunity to use him to do his dirty work and help him towards his obsession of becoming editor of a top news tabloid.

The more news-grabbing front pages he could write, the better, and Michael was certainly supplying them thick and fast.

Tommy told him that God had also spoken to him and had given him a list of people that Michael the Archangel should kill and take their souls for judgment. And so, it all began.

Tommy, working closely with the police, could give all the details to Michael, and Michael had the skills to carry out the killings in the name of God. It had worked perfectly.

"I think we're done here," said Tommy.

Michael stared at Goodie.

Tommy Good felt a flicker of fear run through him.

"What are you going to do, Mick? Kill me as well?"

For a moment, there was tense silence.

Then, Michael got out of the car. As he did so, Tommy spoke.

"I wish you luck if you find Rawlings. He's a slippery customer and a dangerous one."

Michael said nothing as he walked away.

* * *

As Tommy pulled up outside the offices of *The Bristol Eye*, he saw DCI Harry Bowe waiting outside. When the policeman recognised his car, he walked purposely towards it.

The look on Bowe's face disturbed Tommy Good.

Chapter 24

Goodie parked up and got out of his car as Harry approached him.

"Harry, you're the last person I thought I would see. What can I do for you?"

"Can we talk somewhere private?"

"Yeah, sure. Come up to my office."

Both men went inside the building and took the lift to the first floor. The ride didn't take long, but it was an uncomfortable one.

Once in Goodie's office, Harry spoke.

"I read your latest article on the killings."

"What did you think?" replied Goodie.

Harry ignored the question.

"The article told of the killer having a limp on his left leg."

Goodie looked puzzled.

"You've lost me, Harry."

"Then, let me enlighten you. I never revealed that piece of evidence outside of my team for fear of every copycat nutjob contacting us, so how the fuck did you get it?"

Goodie smiled nervously.

"You must have let it slip to me."

Harry shook his head.

"That never happened. Spill it, Goodie. Is one of my team dirty? Are they supplying you with confidential information?"

"Jesus Christ, Harry. No. None of your team are doing that. Honest."

"Then, how did you know?"

"What can I tell you, Harry?" said Goodie.

"Listen, Goodie. You're withholding evidence in the biggest fucking manhunt Bristol and my police department has ever seen. I will arrest you for obstruction. I will paint such a black picture of you that no newspaper will ever want to work with you again. I can promise you that."

Fear flickered in Tommy Good's eyes. He couldn't risk losing the chance of his big break. He had worked too hard for it."

Harry continued.

"I've been doing some thinking on the way over here. When I went to the Vault Gym and was told Michael was working there, he would have had no way of knowing I was coming, but he somehow conveniently did a runner after receiving a phone call. You were the only other person outside my team who I told about my visit. You tipped him off, didn't you?"

"Now, hang on a minute. That's a big accusation, Harry. I..."

Suddenly, a phone rang in Goodie's pocket.

"Why don't you answer that, Tommy?" said Harry.

"No. It can wait."

"It might be important. Go on, I'm not going anywhere."

Harry watched Tommy Good like a hawk.

"Funny that your regular phone is on your desk and not ringing, Tommy. Have another, do you?"

Goodie didn't know what to say.

"Take the phone out, Tommy. Now!" demanded Harry.

Goodie reached into his pocket and took out the pay-as you-go burner. It had stopped ringing, but a text had pinged through.

"Hand it to me."

Goodie handed the phone over. Harry read the text out loud.

I need Rawlings' home address. One last favour. Then I'll be gone out of your life forever

"This is Michael, isn't it? Tell me what's going on, Goodie."

Goodie looked at Harry.

"I can't."

"Then, in that case, you're under arrest."

Tommy Good panicked and tried to run for the door. It really was a kneejerk reaction as he hadn't a clue where he was running to.

Harry grabbed the back of Goodie's collar and jammed his left arm up his back. He swung him around, face first into the desk. Harry easily cuffed him. He then read Goodie out his rights.

* * *

Back at the station in the interview room, Goodie sat with his lawyer. Across the table from him were DCI Bowe and DI Khan.

The burner phone had contained messages back and forth with Michael. The evidence was damning, with

Goodie supplying names, places and times to Michael about all the deceased victims. There was also a record of the call that Michael received that day at the Vault Gym. At the moment, Goodie was looking at accessory to ten counts of murder.

The DCI had the recorder running.

"Tommy, you're in some serious trouble here. If you don't speak to me, I can do nothing to help you. The evidence is overwhelming against you. You will go down for a very long time."

Tommy Good stirred at the table. All his plans had gone up in smoke. He should have ditched the burner phone, but it had slipped his mind.

"It's your right to stay silent, but it won't stop you from going to court," continued Harry, "If there's anything you can tell us to help your case, then this is the time to do it. I promise I'll try to help."

Tommy Good looked up. He saw sincerity in the policeman's eyes. He knew that Harry meant it.

"Okay, Harry."

Harry nodded.

"How do you know this Michael, or should I say Mick Lange?"

"I knew him from childhood. We were brought up in the same neighbourhood and went to the same school. As he got older, it was more and more obvious that I was gay and those were tough times in the 80s to come out as queer. Mick never judged me and stayed my friend. He also looked after me if somebody tried to start trouble. Even back then, he was a tough lad.

As we grew into our teens, Mick expressed a wish to join the army, which he did when he turned sixteen. As for me, I went to university and studied journalism.

We still kept in touch. Mick was close to my sister Angela. When they were young, they had a teenage crush on each other, but it never really went anywhere.

Not long after Mick joined the army, he lost his parents in a car crash. This brought Mick, Angela and I even closer. Angela later got married and had a boy. Joe. Eventually, Joe joined the army and ended up by pure coincidence in Mick's team in the SAS. Mick promised us that he would look after Joe and get him back from Afghanistan safely.

Something happened on a mission out there and Mick's team were ambushed. They all died, including Joe. Mick somehow survived and made it back to safety, but he was badly wounded. In hospital, he apparently died on the operating table for two minutes, but eventually pulled through.

After that, we never heard anything from him for years. He seemed to have disappeared off the face of the earth. Then, about three months ago, he just called me out of the blue. He asked if he could visit Angela and me. I told him that Angela had recently taken her own life, not being able to cope with the fact that her only son was dead. She never got over it and she blamed Mick for not keeping his promise. It was harsh of her, but she would not change her mind. Mick was already guilt ridden about Joe's death. Now, he had Angela's on his conscience too.

He visited and told me his whole story. The incident in Afghanistan, his medical discharge from the SAS and his subsequent spell in prison. The strangest thing he told me was about his near-death experience on the operating table where he said that he was walking in a corridor of light to heaven and that he had spoken to

God. God had supposedly told him that he couldn't die yet and had to go back to do his work. He told him he was no longer Mick Lange, but Michael the Archangel and that he now worked for the Almighty collecting souls for retribution."

Harry interrupted Tommy Good.

"Did you believe him?"

"Hell no. I'm not a religious man. I believe he was suffering severe PTSD and terrible guilt from the death of Joe. I think he convinced himself that he had a new purpose in life and one that would absolve him. Working for God as a spiritual warrior."

"So, then what?" asked Harry.

"I saw an opportunity. Firstly, to rid our city's streets of the scum that was clogging it up. Criminals giving you the runaround and who knew how to play the legal system. I've reported as long as I can remember about these lowlifes getting away with offence after offence. Now, I had somebody in front of me more than equipped to deal with this problem and was practically begging for a sign from God to do it.

So, I convinced him that I had also had a vision from God and I was his go-between. I could supply the souls and Mick, or Michael as he was now known, could take them. That was how it began. Through reporting and working closely with the police, I knew all the scum and their whereabouts. It was easy.

The other motivation was that I was now writing big, exclusive and sensational headlines that would get me noticed and hopefully get me a prime job with one of the top tabloids. I'm too good a journalist to be wasted with a local rag such as *The Bristol Eye*. Reporting daily on traffic offences, missing cats and our shit football teams.

I want bigger and better, and Michael, or 'The Avenging Angel' as I eventually coined him, was going to get me that fame. It was a win, win situation."

Harry leant forward in his seat.

"So, all the time my team and I have been busting our balls trying to piece together and find this killer, you knew who he was."

Tommy smiled wryly.

"I'm afraid I did. I'm sorry for that Harry. I know what a dedicated copper you are, but let's face it… you couldn't put these criminals behind bars. God knows you tried enough. But with the help of Michael, I saw to it that they got their comeuppance. Don't tell me you can't see that. The crime figures have dropped drastically over the last few months. Instead of putting me away, you could be calling the mayor to give me a fucking medal."

Harry shook his head.

"You selfish, deluded fool, Goodie. What have you done?"

Tommy Good sat back in his chair, somewhat puzzled. He thought that he had produced a very good case for himself. One that he was prepared to bring to court and stand by. The public would see him as a hero, not a villain. Surely.

"Is Michael going after Charlie Rawlings?" asked Harry.

"I believe so. He told me that was his final soul for taking here in Bristol before leaving," replied Goodie.

"Do you know where he's at now?"

Goodie shook his head.

"No. Sorry, I don't. But one thing I know, he's hellbent on finding Rawlings."

Harry switched off the tape.

"DS Khan, take Mr Good here back to his cell."

As Good and his lawyer stood up, the journalist looked at Harry.

"Are we good here, Harry? Can you help me out? I told you all I know."

Harry turned and left the room.

Outside, he found his way to the bathroom, went to the sink and splashed some cold water on his face. He had run himself into the ground on this case and all along Goodie had known the killer and had continued on his crazy campaign while also pretending to help the police.

Tomorrow was Christmas Eve. He now needed to get all his team out on the streets tracking down Rawlings before Michael found him.

On impulse, he went back into the interview room and saw the burner phone in the plastic evidence bag left by his file. Harry reached into his pocket and pulled out a pair of surgical gloves. He slipped them on, took out the phone and opened up the address book.

He found Michael's phone number and rang it. After a few rings, it was answered.

"Goodie, did you get my text?" said a voice on the other end.

"This isn't Goodie, Michael. This is DCI Harry Bowe. Tommy Good is in custody. He's told us it all. It's over. Hand yourself in and I can help you. I know your background. There are mitigating circumstances to what you did. I can get you help, but you must stop the killing and come in."

There was a moment of silence. Then, Michael spoke.

"I've been told about you, Chief Inspector, and how dogged you are to catch your man. I admire that. I truly do. You're a dying breed. You know I have to finish my mission. I'm also dogged. Once I have, though, you won't hear of me again here in Bristol. I'll be gone. Give me that respect, Chief Inspector. You know the people I've murdered were vile scum, so is Rawlings. The world will be a better place without them. Your job will be better without them. Deep down, you know that."

"There may be truth in what you say, but I've sworn to uphold the truth and to do my job. If you don't hand yourself in, then I'm coming for you, Michael."

"I understand, Chief Inspector. Now you understand, I'm doing God's will, the highest authority in the universe, and I'm not going to let him down. So, if you're coming, I'll be ready for you. I really don't want to have to kill you, but if you stop me from my mission, I will. Goodbye, Chief Inspector."

The phone clicked off.

Harry sat in silence for some time replaying the conversation, before returning the phone to the bag and bringing it to be stored for evidence.

Chapter 25

Christmas Eve

Charlie Rawlings was in the Vault Gym. It was late morning. The gym was shut to the public, but he had gathered his trusted top boys from the firm together and had put them clearly in the picture about this man called Michael and what he had done to Leroy Curtis.

The three men standing in the gym with Rawlings were loyal and trusted lieutenants. Gerry Tucker, Ian Broughton and Charlie's brother Dennis.

Owner Ed Lyons had given them some space. He had never seen Charlie so worked up. When he was in this sort of mood, he stayed well clear of him. This Michael guy had well and truly put the wind up Rawlings.

All the men sat around a boxing ring, which stood in the far corner of the gym. Rawlings had dished out shooters to everybody.

"Right. This bastard is coming, make no mistake. He'll find out my home address and any other places I hang out. He knows this gym well. We can't let him get the advantage. We need to be ready for him when he shows up. You shoot to kill and then get rid of the gun. I want nothing coming back on me. Understand?"

The men nodded.

Ed poked his head around the gym door.

"More coffee, boys? Or do you fancy something stronger?"

"We'll stick to the coffee. There'll be time to celebrate when we bring this bastard down."

"Are you sure he hasn't just gone, Charlie?" asked Dennis.

"No. We hurt the old priest badly and he seemed close to him. I don't see him as the forgiving sort. He'll want revenge for what we did. Leroy has already paid the price. Now he wants me."

The men looked nervously at each other. Nobody would tell Charlie to his face, but they were worried.

They all knew how to handle themselves in a fight and none were strangers to a bit of torture or gratuitous violence when needed, but going up against some ex-SAS soldier with a screw loose was another story.

Leroy Curtis had been a ferocious man, but he had been cut down like nothing.

They had all read in the newspapers and online about what this Michael had done to all his victims. This man was a killing machine. Maybe they were out of their depth?

They rationalised that strength was in numbers. Plus, they were all armed.

"So, what's the plan? We can't hole up in here all Christmas," said Gerry Tucker.

"The plan is this…" answered Charlie, "I believe he may attempt to visit the priest. I hear the old boy is at death's door. It's Christmas Eve. After today, he'll find it difficult to get in to visit anybody. He needs to blend into the crowd.

Christmas Day and Boxing Day, there's gonna be skeleton staff and restricted visits. Visiting hours today are 2:00pm to 4:00pm and 6:00pm to 8:00pm. Dennis, you and Ian go keep an eye on the priest. Be careful as the police have somebody on the door of his room. Gerry, you go down to the haulage yard and make sure all is well there and shut up for the holiday break at 5:00pm.

My festive period is gonna be lowkey this year. Like non-existent. I can't even chance going to visit Duane. The police are bound to be looking for me too. When this is over and the Albanian deal is squared away, then that visit to the villa in Spain is looking ever more inviting. I'm going to see if an old friend will put me up for a few days. I'll call if I need you guys."

"Charlie, will you be okay on your own?" asked Ian Broughton.

"If this fucker wants me, he can come and get me. I'm not letting this joker worry me. I'm Charlie Rawlings. I'll crush this man. I have a reputation to uphold. I can't and won't let this Michael character mess with that or hold me to ransom.

I thought the right thing was to bring big Leroy down here to sort him. I didn't want any blood on my hands, but that proved a mistake. Now, I have no choice, but to deal with him myself. If you want a job doing and all that bollocks. Anyway, I'm gonna enjoy Christmas the best I can in some good company. I'm gonna stay with Ruby."

The men all got up and headed for the door. Ed was just coming in with more coffees.

"Sorry, Ed. We have to be on our way. Once we've gone, shut the place up and enjoy the Christmas," said Charlie.

"If you need anything from me, just ring," replied Ed.

* * *

Ed watched the men go and shut the door, locking it securely. He would exit by the side door after putting the alarm on.

He returned the tray of coffee mugs to the small kitchen, washed them up and left them to dry on the draining board.

He was looking forward to a few days off and spending it with his wife Karen and daughter Zoe.

He now went back into the main gym to switch off the lights and was surprised to see a treadmill running. Maybe one of the lads had been messing around on it and forgot to turn it off?

Ed walked over to it and switched it off. He turned around and was startled to see Michael standing there holding a heavy black gun on him.

"You. How did you get in here?" said Ed, warily eying the weapon.

"You should always regularly check the outside of your premises. You've had a busted window catch around in the car park for weeks. Handy to get in and out undetected," answered Michael.

"What do you want?"

"Simple really, Ed. I want Charlie's Rawlings home address, please."

Ed laughed.

"You have some neck. You can go to hell," said Ed.

Michael saw defiance in the older man's eyes. He had to admire that.

"Ed, I like you, but I'm running out of time. Tell me. It won't make any difference to you. There'll be no comeback cos he'll be dead."

"Charlie is a friend. I'm not going to give him up. You're getting nothing from me."

"So, you're willing to die for Rawlings, are you?" asked Michael, "But what about your daughter Zoe, is she?"

Ed's face changed from defiance to concern.

"What about my daughter.? You better not have touched her."

"She's safe for now, but if you want to spend Christmas with her, you better give me that address."

Ed then smiled.

"You're bluffing. You haven't got her."

"Why not ring her? She was meant to be at home today. Home being 34 Headley Park Road. Am I right?"

The smile faded from the older man's face as he dug his phone out of his pocket and pressed his daughter's number. He let it ring for a dozen times or more with no reply.

Ed now looked at Michael.

"You bastard. What have you done to her?"

Michael levelled the gun on Ed.

"Like I said, she's safe for now and I'll release her unharmed. Now, give me what I want. You know what I've already done to those people, and you know what I'm capable of. I have nothing left to lose."

"Alright, you crazy bastard. I'll give you the address. It's Apartment A, Waterside View, the city docks," said Ed.

"Thank you. Now, give me your phone."

"What? Why?" asked Ed.

"Because I don't want you ringing Rawlings as soon as I leave."

Ed reached in his pocket and took out his phone. He walked towards Michael and handed it to him. As he did so, he made a grab for the gun. Michael retracted it safely and then struck the older man on the side of the jaw, using the butt of the weapon. The result was Ed dropping to the ground stunned.

"That was stupid. You could have got yourself killed."

Michael put the phone in his pocket and then bent down to the fallen man.

"Your daughter is out in the car park. She's bound and in the red dumpster."

As Michael walked off, Ed called out.

"Why didn't you take the opportunity to kill him earlier when he was here? Why let him go?"

Michael stopped and turned back.

"Because I would have had to kill the other three men and you. I want to avoid that. My job is to kill Charlie Rawlings. Period. No more killings after. It's God's wish."

Ed looked at the man, who seemed perfectly sane.

"Who the fuck are you, mister?"

"I'm Michael the Archangel."

Michael then left the gym the same way that he came in: through the broken window.

Chapter 26

Harry had the whole team out on the streets. It was snowing heavily, yet the roads and pavements were busy with cars and pedestrians. Everybody had some work to finish or a last-minute present to buy as Christmas Day got ever closer.

Harry, along with DS Khan, had gone to Rawlings' dockside department. To get to it, you had to access a privately owned underground car park, which would then bring you up in a lift to the various apartments with fabulous views out over the harbour.

Harry marvelled at how Rawlings got the money to buy one of these. He did run a legitimate haulage company, which was a convenient front for his other nefarious business interests.

Who said crime doesn't pay?

* * *

When they reached Apartment A and buzzed the intercom, there was no response.

Harry knew that Rawlings also had a more downmarket flat in Bedminster to keep his street cred. His haulage yard was also in the same area.

Members of his team were at those locations, as well as Max's Snooker Hall and the Vault Gym.

There was no sign of Rawlings at any of them or any of his cronies.

There was no sign of Michael either.

"Okay, Ali. I want you to stay here and stake out the apartment. If you see Rawlings, contact me immediately," said Bowe, "I'm heading back to the office."

"Okay, guv. Understood."

As Harry went back to his car, his phone rang and he saw that it was his wife Carol calling.

He answered immediately.

"Hello, love. Everything alright?"

"Yes, I thought you'd like to know as soon as possible that Father Matthew is being discharged from hospital and going to a rest home to recover. He's a lot better, but still weak. The address is Elm Tree Care Home Trust, 48 Capel Road, Fairfield, Gloucester. The trust specialises in care for ill or retired clergy. He'll be safe there. Apparently, a stand-in priest will run the parish in his absence. He started today."

"Is the church open again?"

"Yes, they needed to get it up and running again for the Christmas season."

"Thanks for the heads up. Much appreciated."

"What time do you finish today?" asked Harry.

"All being well, my shift ends at 9:00pm. Will you be home for dinner?"

Carol knew that it was a speculative question.

"Maybe a late supper. I'll keep you posted."

"Okay, love. I'll see you later."

"Will do."

"Oh, Harry... and be careful, will you?"

For the first time in an age, Harry heard apprehension in his wife's voice.

"Are you okay, Carol?"

"Yes. I just feel a little uneasy about this whole case you're working on."

"I'll be fine. Once I sew it up, I promise we'll head off to a sunnier climate for a well-earnt break."

"I'll hold you to that, DCI Bowe. I had Spain in mind. There's still some sun over there this time of year."

"And there I was thinking of Weston-super-Mare."

Harry cut the call, before he heard his wife's response.

***

Harry's mind now went back to the job.

He knew that if he found Charlie, he had a good chance of finding Michael. He sensed that the man was not going to leave Bristol until he settled the score with Rawlings. By the same token, Rawlings was not the sort of man to run away. He had a big reputation to uphold. His whole nasty little empire rested on it.

Earlier, the body of the black man murdered in the church was revealed as Leroy Denzil Curtis, 35 years of age residing in Newcastle upon Tyne. He had a string of convictions for violence. Harry deduced that Rawling had hired him to eliminate Michael, but it had all gone pear-shaped.

Harry couldn't help, but grudgingly tip his hat to Michael. He was like John Rambo and the Terminator rolled into one. No wonder the SAS were revered and toted as the world's best fighting unit.

Sadly, this soldier was badly flawed. His hardwiring had been tampered with. He believed that he was some crusader for God with a free license to kill and this made him very dangerous and highly unpredictable.

Tommy Good had taken advantage of this fact for his own selfish ends. Fortunately, he was stopped, but not before much bloodshed and death had come to Harry's city.

He had to make sure that there would be no more.

Chapter 27

Charlie Rawlings rolled over and reached for his cigarettes by the bedside.

"Want one?" he asked the blonde-haired woman next to him in bed.

Her name was Ruby Webber. She had been Charlie's on/off girlfriend for several years now. She was an ex-Page Three model from back in the day, although she never reached the heights and fame of Samantha Fox or Katie Price. Still, she had earnt herself some decent money and had still kept her looks, even though she was now in her late forties.

Ruby had no shortage of male attention. Most were businessmen, who lavished her with riches. She had a soft spot for Charlie, though, having grown up together in the Bristol area.

At one time, they could have been an item, but Charlie only had eyes for his wife-to-be Cathy. Cathy had tragically died giving birth to Duane. Charlie was devastated. He loved her unconditionally. She was the only person that could really control him and bring out his gentler side.

When Cathy died, he could have gone off the deep end, but he had a son to look after. With the help of his mum and her sister, the boy got cared for the best he could, but inevitably, he was drawn into his father's life of crime.

The apple doesn't fall very far from the tree.

Charlie never talked about Cathy. It was like a part of his life that he had stored away. Ruby knew better than to ask him about it.

A few years after his wife's death, Charlie and Ruby had met up in a pub. Both got drunk and spoke about childhood and days gone by. They had clicked with one another and, that night, they had ended up in bed together. Neither wanted a heavy relationship, so they just kept to this casual agreement.

Ruby had to admit that she was surprised to see Charlie on her doorstep and even more surprised that he asked if he could spend Christmas with her. She welcomed the company as all her gentlemen friends would be playing happy families at home with their wives and kids.

Ruby took the offered cigarette.

"I heard your Duane is inside."

"Yeah. He did something stupid. He rang me earlier and I wished him a happy Christmas. What sort of Christmas is the boy gonna have behind bars?" replied Charlie.

"He knows you love him, Charlie. Maybe that's enough to get him through it."

Charlie pulled back the duvet and got out of bed.

"Maybe."

He walked to the bathroom.

"I'm gonna grab a shower. I could murder another drink."

***

Come late afternoon, the police team were getting despondent. There was no sign of Rawlings at any of his usual places. They were beginning to think that he had gone away for Christmas or maybe that's what he wanted everybody to think.

Back at the office, Harry had wracked his brain, thinking of Rawlings' whereabouts. He pulled out Rawlings' file. It was as thick as a brick. He began to read through it. Maybe there was a clue to his location in there somewhere.

After an hour, he came across something.

Going back a few years ago, Rawlings was in the frame for the murder of a drugdealer, Quentin Lomas, but he had a cast iron alibi at the time from a girlfriend called Ruby Webber. She told him that he was with her all night and the police had no evidence to suggest otherwise. Harry knew that the girl had been lying, but as was so often the case these days, he was powerless to do anything about it.

Could Rawlings be holed up with her again seeking shelter?

He looked at the address. 33 Long Green Terrace, Clifton.

Harry knew the affluent area of Bristol. The ex-model had done well for herself. It was worth a shot.

Harry rang DS Rose and asked her to come and pick him up from the station. They would drive over to Ruby Webber's place together. He might need a bit of female support if Ruby kicked off.

* * *

Michael watched the haulage yard and saw the lone man begin to walk around the place checking it. It looked like he was getting ready to close up.

He had been to the dockside flat, but saw a police car parked up outside waiting there. That told him that it was unlikely that Rawlings was at home.

Not far down the road, he spotted a van with an advertisement on the side for Rawlings Haulage and an address of the business. He thought that this might be worth a try.

Michael moved across the road to the open gate and watched the man disappear into a site office. He drew his Glock and entered the yard.

He crept up the steps to the site office door. On peeking through the window, he saw the man sat at a desk going through some files. He looked a typical heavy. The kind of man used to violence and no doubt loyal to his boss. Maybe.

Michael decided a Route 1 entry was the only way to go, so he kicked open the door and rushed in. Ian Broughton looked up in surprise and dropped the file that he had in his hands.

Michael levelled the gun at his head.

"I'm going to ask you once and once only. Where's Charlie Rawlings?"

Broughton raised his hands.

"I don't know. Honest. I'm just shutting the yard up for him."

Michael fired the gun.

The bullet whizzed past Broughton's head, taking half of his ear with him. The man fell back off his chair to the floor, howling in pain as he clutched the side of his head.

Michael walked around the desk and levelled the gun again.

"Is Rawlings worth dying for? Think about it seriously. If I fire again, it's curtains for you."

Broughton shuffled back on his ass to lean against the filing cabinet.

"I saw him earlier at the Vault Gym, but he isn't there now. He asked me to lock up the yard. He went off on his own."

"Where would he go if he wanted to lie low for a while?"

"I don't know. He could be anywhere."

Michael aimed the gun between Broughton's eyes.

"Think."

Panic showed on the man's face.

"Alright, alright. He might be at an old girlfriend's flat. A Ruby Webber."

"Give me the address and don't fuck me about," said Michael.

Broughton gave him it.

"There. That wasn't so bad, was it?" Michael exclaimed.

He then threw a hard right hook onto the man's jaw, knocking him unconscious.

Michael ripped out the landline phone and threw Broughton's mobile out of the door. He then locked the office door from the outside and threw the key away. Armed with the address, he jumped in the transit and headed there.

Chapter 28

Rawlings took a pull on the spliff, then sipped on a glass of champagne and scrolled through his phone. There were no latest headlines on the murders.

Suddenly, his phone rang. He saw it was his brother Dennis. He answered it.

"Yes, Dennis?"

"Just to let you know, the priest has been discharged from hospital. Do you want us to stay here?"

Rawlings thought about it.

"No. I don't see this Michael character going there now. Call it a day. Even psychotic bastards must take a day off for Christmas."

Charlie was feeling mellow and relaxed from the cocktail of drugs and booze.

"I'm at Ruby's flat. Pop over about 8:00pm with Gerry if you want for a drink, seeing as it's Christmas. Ruby is off out with a few mates, so we'll have the place to ourselves."

"Nice one, Charlie. I'll see you later. I'll bring a few bottles."

Ruby came into the bedroom from the shower. She was dressed in just a fluffy pink towel.

"Hungry, babe?" she asked.

"Always for you, darling" replied Charlie.

Ruby rolled her eyes.

"No. I meant food, you randy sod."

"Yeah, starving."

"I'll send out for a couple of pizzas. What do you think?"

"Spot on. I'll have a meat feast, please."

Ruby left the bedroom, looking for her phone.

Charlie lay back on the bed and closed his eyes. He would be alright here for a few days. Keep his head down away from the cops and this lunatic. Then, he would flush the bastard out. For now, he would chill.

Ruby was a great girl, but she could take it out of you at times. Charlie wasn't as young as he used to be anymore.

* * *

Michael got out of the van and looked up the street. It was quiet and strangely silent due to the fall of snow. It wasn't going to be a country-stopping fall, but it just made things seem muted.

He checked his weapons under his coat. He was ready.

Walking up the road stealthily, he regarded the house numbers. 25. 26. 27.

Suddenly, a noise filled the air and a motorbike appeared on the street. Michael slipped into the cover of some trees in a driveway.

The bike came to a halt a few houses up from where he stood. A figure got off, went to the box on the back of the bike and opened it. A minute later, he pulled out a couple of pizza boxes.

Michael watched, hardly believing his luck. Where these pizzas going to number 33? He had to take a chance that they were.

Michael began walking up the street and caught up with the pizza delivery on the steps of 33.

"Excuse me. Are those for Ruby Webber, number 33?"

The delivery person was startled.

"Yes, they are."

The voice behind the full-face crash helmet was female.

Michael smiled.

"Great. I thought I was gonna be late. I hate cold pizza. I'll take them on from here."

The girl kept hold of the delivery.

"Sorry, but I need to deliver them personally."

"It's fine. I'm Ruby's boyfriend. Look, it's Christmas Eve and I'm sure you would rather be home out of this snow. So, here. Merry Christmas."

Michael handed over a twenty-pound note.

The girl regarded it like it was a diamond ring. She tentatively took it and passed over the pizzas.

"Thank you."

Michael smiled.

"No worries. It'll be our secret. Have a great Christmas."

He watched as the girl walked back down the steps, got back on the bike and started it up. As she went to pull away, she looked back at Michael, who gave her a friendly wave.

When she had disappeared, Michael drew the Glock and rang the bell.

He prepared himself. Adrenaline was coursing through his veins like a speeding bullet.

***

Ruby heard the doorbell ring.

"I'll get it, Charlie. It's the pizzas."

Charlie woke up. He must have dozed off. He sat up with a start.

"Just a minute, Ruby. Let me go."

Panic washed over him. The combination of good sex, good champagne and cannabis had dulled his senses. He needed to make sure that it was the pizza delivery. Just in case...

* * *

Ruby headed to the front door.

"Yes. Who is it?" she called.

"Pizza delivery," came the reply.

Ruby opened the front door and Michael pushed his way in. Dropping the pizzas, he grabbed Ruby as she screamed.

Charlie Rawlings stepped out of the bedroom and ran down the hallway, just as he saw Ruby open the door. He then saw a figure push their way in. He also saw the gun.

Michael had somehow found him.

He raised his own gun, but the man had grabbed Ruby and was using her as a shield.

"Drop the gun, Rawlings, or I'll put a bullet in the girl's head," said Michael.

Rawlings froze.

"I said, lose the gun," repeated Michael.

Charlie Rawlings slowly began to lower his weapon.

"Okay, buddy. Take it easy. There's no need to hurt the girl. You've found me. It's me you want, not her."

Charlie brought the gun to his side. It looked for all the world like he was going to drop it, but he suddenly raised it again sharply and let off a shot at Michael.

The shot was ill judged.

The bullet hit Ruby in the neck.

The force knocked her and Michael backwards. Blood erupted from the fatal wound.

Michael let the girl go. Her body collapsed to the ground.

Rawlings momentarily paused, realising his grave error.

Michael fired back as Rawlings fired again.

Both bullets found their targets.

Michael was hit in the right shoulder, while Rawlings took a slug to the abdomen.

Rawlings staggered back into the wall and fired off another round. His bullet caught Michael also in the stomach.

Michael fired off another round and his bullet hit Rawlings squarely in the chest. Charlie Rawlings slid down the wall, still firing but his shots now falling short of the mark.

Then, the gun was empty.

Rawlings watched Michael walk towards him and then stand over him.

Through gritted teeth, Rawlings spoke.

"Go on then, you crazy fuck. Finish it. That's what you came for, so do it. Come on!"

Michael regarded the man.

"Time for your soul to be delivered to hell."

Michael took aim and put a bullet straight between Rawlings' eyes.

Suddenly, he heard footfalls running up the steps. Two men were framed in the doorway.

Michael raised his gun.

***

Dennis Rawlings and Gerry Tucker stood in the doorway of 33 Long Green Terrace. They had both heard shots as they had pulled up in their car.

Just inside the hallway, they saw the dead body of Ruby Webber in an ever-expanding pool of blood. A bullet wound had ripped her neck apart.

Down the hall was the still bloodied body of Charlie Rawlings. Standing over him was a figure of a big man dressed head to toe in black. In his left hand was the unmistakable shape of a Glock pistol.

The smell of blood and cordite hung heavy in the air.

Dennis Rawlings roared in pain and anger at the sight of his beloved older brother. He ran down the hallway towards the man in black, reaching at the same time into his coat pocket for his own gun.

Michael levelled his gun and fired two rapid shots. Both hit Dennis squarely in the chest, instantly putting him down.

Michael now levelled the gun at the other man, who stood frozen like a statue in the doorway.

"I'll let you live if you turn around and walk now," said Michael.

Gerry Tucker slowly raised his hands.

"Okay, mister. I'm going. I no longer want any part of this."

Michael watched the man leave. He now walked into the living room and slumped into the armchair. He was losing blood and felt slightly woozy. He needed medical attention.

Opening his coat, he looked at the stomach wound. It didn't look good.

For a moment, he was transported back to that night in Afghanistan, lying wounded watching his team die around him.

For a few moments, he shut his eyes and then he was aware of somebody entering the room.

He opened his eyes.

The man who had left was back and brandishing a gun.

Gerry Tucker spoke.

"I had to come back. Those are my friends you wasted. I couldn't walk away."

Michael nodded.

"I know."

Tucker gestured with his gun.

"Drop the Glock."

Michael slowly let the gun slip from his fingers to the carpet.

Tucker smiled.

"It's time for payback. For all the shit you've done."

As Tucker came forward, Michael reached for the Browning automatic he had put between his legs when he had sat down on the chair. Something had told him that this man would be back.

Tucker didn't even see the gun until a bullet slammed into his chest, stopping him in his tracks. The look of pure surprise was wiped away as another bullet ploughed through his face and entered his brain.

Michael slowly got up, walked over to the dead man and searched in his pockets, finding a set of car keys.

He left the house and saw a blue BMW parked directly outside. He pressed the key fob and the car's lights flashed as the doors opened. Unsteadily, he managed to get in the driver's seat, started up the car and headed for the nearest hospital.

Chapter 29

The journey across the city to Clifton was proving to be a difficult one due to the snowy conditions and heavy evening traffic.

DI Rose drove the Volvo expertly through the traffic as Harry looked out the passenger side window. He had a feeling about this hunch. The more he thought about it, the more he was convinced that Rawlings had gone to ground at Ruby Webber's house. The likelihood of Michael finding him there was slim, to say the least.

His thoughts were abruptly interrupted by his phone ringing. He fished it out of his coat pocket and saw DS Jim Leech was calling. He pressed the button and answered.

"Yes, Jim. What have you got?"

"Guv, I'm at another crime scene and it looks like our boy has been busy again."

Harry's stomach lurched.

"Where are you, Jim?"

Before Jim spoke, Harry had a horrible feeling that he knew the answer to his own question.

"I'm at the property of a Ms Ruby Webber, 33 Long Green Terrace, Clifton. Neighbours reported hearing what sounded like gun shots about half an hour ago. We have four bodies and one of them is Charlie Rawlings."

Harry was stunned. How the hell did Michael find Rawlings and how did he get inside the house to murder him?

"Who are the other three dead?" he asked.

"Ruby Webber, Dennis Rawlings and we think a Gerry Tucker, although half his head is missing."

"Is the scene secure, Jim?"

"Yes, guv. Myself and DC Stewart have it covered."

"Okay, Jim. Ironically, I was on my way there to speak to Ruby Webber. I guess that's out of the equation now. I'll be there shortly anyway."

Harry hung up and related the news to DI Rose.

"Better get the siren on, Diane, and put your foot down."

Suddenly, Christmas Eve had just got longer.

* * *

Michael pulled up outside A&E at Southfields Hospital.

He staggered out of the car. The pain he was now experiencing was excruciating. He felt like he was going to pass out at any moment.

He walked through the sliding doors of the A&E department and promptly collapsed on the floor.

* * *

Harry stood in the cold, watching the bodies being taken out to the coroner's van.

The crime scene had been like a Wild West shootout.

All the victims were dead.

Charlie Rawlings' reign was over and, with his son banged up, his empire was crumbling.

Harry had to admit that he would not shed any tears for this violent man.

It had been tragic that Ruby had probably died in the crossfire, though. She had really only been guilty of loving a dangerous and manipulating criminal.

What interested Harry the most was that the scenes of crime guys had found a trail of blood leading out of the house and down the steps to the pavement. Then, the trail stopped.

If it was Michael's blood, as expected, he must have got into a car, but he must have sustained an injury himself.

DI Rose came up to her boss.

"What now, sir? Do you think it's all over and the killings will stop?"

"I don't know, Diane. The only thing I do know is Bristol has seen enough bloodshed in the last few months and I haven't been able to stop it. This Michael was always one step ahead of the game due to Goodie's input."

"You can't be too hard on yourself, sir. We all failed collectively as a team."

Harry nodded.

"That may be true, but it'll be my balls on the chopping block."

Harry smiled grimly.

"Anyway, time you got home and enjoyed some of the festivities. Merry Christmas, Diane."

Diane Rose lightly touched Harry's arm.

"And Merry Christmas to you, gov."

* * *

Harry watched DI Rose pull away.

He turned back to the house. So much for the season of good will to all men.

He then felt his phone vibrate in his pocket. Fishing it out, he saw that it was his wife calling. He would have to break the news that he probably wasn't going to be home tonight by the time he had written up his report.

"Hello, Carol. Are you okay?"

When Carol spoke, he could sense excitement and trepidation in her voice.

"Harry, a man just walked into A&E and collapsed on the floor. He has gunshot wounds and, by his look and dress, I think it's your killer."

Harry felt his heart leap.

"Where is he now?"

"He's in theatre undergoing an operation to remove the bullets."

"Will he live?"

"He's lost a lot of blood from a stomach wound. It'll be touch and go."

"Right, I'm on my way."

Harry looked around and spotted Jim Leech.

"Jim, I need to borrow your car urgently."

Jim Leech reached in his pocket and grabbed his keys, handing them over to his superior.

"Everything alright, guv?"

"Everything might be fucking great, Jim. You're now in charge of this scene. Wrap it up here when you're done."

* * *

When Harry got to the hospital, he found Carol, who informed him that the operation was over and the man was in ICU recovering. He wouldn't be speaking anytime soon.

Harry was frustrated, but knew that he could do nothing about it. At least, he now had his man where he wanted him.

Harry asked if he could go and see Michael.

Carol went off to seek permission.

She returned and told Harry that he had five minutes with the patient.

Harry found his way to ICU and was brought to room four where Michael was.

The DCI looked through the window.

Lying in bed was a big man with dark hair and a couple of days growth of beard. Various tubes were sticking out of him, and a machine bleeped away by the bedside.

So, this was the man called Michael the Avenging Angel.

Harry couldn't believe that he had finally caught up with the elusive killer.

This man was a broken product of the Forces. A loose cannon. A man who had once been a captain in the SAS and a decorated veteran had somehow slipped through the system.

He had severe mental health problems, the byproduct of PTSD from the horrors of war.

Captain Mick Lange had somehow convinced himself that he was Michael the Archangel whose mission was to take souls for God.

As damaged and flawed as the man was – and Harry had great empathy for him – this man had also made

John Rambo look like Ghandi. He had to be arrested and charged with multiple murders and then be incarcerated in an institution to see if they could help him.

Reality said that this man would never come out of the system ever again.

What a tragedy.

* * *

Harry walked back to A&E and managed to grab five minutes with Carol before her shift ended.

"Did the CCTV pick up Michael's arrival?" asked Harry.

"Yes, it should have. The car he pulled up in is still out the front. A blue BMW."

"I'll phone Jim Leech now and get him to send some of the team and forensics over here to check it out."

Once he had made the call, Harry took a sip of coffee and pulled a face.

Carol smiled.

"You think that's bad, you should try the tomato soup."

"I'll give it a miss."

Harry then asked.

"Did he have any ID on him when his clothes were removed?"

Carol shook her head.

"No. Nothing. All his pockets were empty."

"That figures," said Harry.

"But…" added Carol, "He was wearing two dogtags. We have them bagged with his clothes. The name on them read Captain Mick Lange. I recalled the name from the newspaper and that really convinced me we had your man."

Harry leant over and kissed Carol.

"You're a star. You may well have helped solve this case. Great detective work, if I may say so."

"Why thank you, DCI Bowe."

Carol dropped her half-drunk coffee cup in the bin.

"Well, time for me to get home and grab a few hours' sleep. It'll soon be Christmas Day."

"Okay, love. Drive safely. The weather isn't great out there. I'll be back…"

Carol interrupted him.

"When you're back. Don't worry. Just wrap this case up."

Harry smiled.

"I'll do my best."

Harry watched Carol walk away. Once again, as he did so often, he thanked the Lord for having such a wonderful wife. When some days the job weighed heavily down on him, she was always that positive ray of light that bucked him up and inspired him to get on with things.

Harry now saw two police cars and a scenes of crime van pull up outside. A minute later, he saw Jim Leech get out of one of the police cars. He looked tired. DC Kenny Stewart now joined him. Out of the other car came DS Ali Khan and DC Mira Sharma.

Harry went out to meet them and put them in the picture.

The look of relief and excitement was apparent on all their faces. This had been a tough time for all involved.

Harry now went inside to give Superintendent Bradley a call. This would make the old bastard's Christmas for sure.

Bradley answered on the first ring. Harry could hear music and people talking in the background. It looked like his boss was at a party.

"Hello, Harry. What have you got for me? I take it this is not a social call to wish me a happy Christmas."

Bradley sounded relaxed, possibly a few glasses of Chablis too many.

"We have him, sir. We've got Mick Lange, aka Michael. He's under observation in Southfields Hospital recovering from bullet wounds. I'm waiting for him to come around to talk to him, but we have him safe and sound."

"Fucking hell. Great work, Harry."

Harry went on to explain the evening's events concerning Charlie Rawlings and co. Bradley listened quietly until Harry had brought him up to speed.

"You have this all under control, Harry?"

"Yes, sir. My team and I are on it until we make that arrest."

This seemed to satisfy Bradley.

"Good man. Once again, congratulations. This certainly is an added Christmas bonus. You've done well, Harry. I never doubted you."

Harry went to remind Bradley that he had thought that one of his team had been a grass until Goodie was arrested, but decided to let it go for now. It was the season of good will after all.

"Thank you, sir. Have a good Christmas."

Harry rang off.

He now saw Jim Leech approach him.

"A preliminary search of the vehicle revealed two guns in the back seat, both recently fired, as well as a couple of knives and an expandable baton. Looks like his arsenal of weapons. All being taking for examination as we speak.

The car is registered to Dennis Rawlings. Blood samples and fingerprints have also been taken, along with DNA. CCTV has been checked and it has picked up the car driving in and this Michael character getting out and heading to A&E. We pretty much have him banged to rights, guv."

"Good work, Jim. I'm staying here until he comes around from the op."

"Need some company, guv?"

"Thanks, Jim, but get home to your family. You've done enough tonight."

"Okay. Thank you. What about the rest of the team?"

"They can go as well, but tell DS Stewart to come in. I'll get him up to Michael's room to keep watch over him."

"Will do, guv. Good night and Merry Christmas."

Harry then received a call from DS Carrie French, who had been manning the office with DC Bailey.

"Sir, I thought I would just give you an update before I go off duty. Mr Patel is out of intensive care and it looks like he'll make a full recovery. Duane Rawlings and his buddies are lucky. They won't be facing murder charges, but will all be doing time for their crime."

"Thanks, Carrie."

"I hear congratulations are in order, sir."

"I believe they are, but that goes for all the team. I wouldn't have been able to do it without you guys. Pass that onto Rob, will you?"

"Thank you, sir. Will do. Have a good Christmas."

"You too, Carrie."

Harry wandered off down the corridor to get another coffee.

Yes, it was like battery acid, but he needed a hit of caffeine to stay awake. It was going to be a long night.

Chapter 30

Harry felt a tap on his shoulder and a voice say 'Sir'. He hadn't realised that he had nodded off in the chair he had been sat on.

He opened his eyes to look up at DC Kenny Stewart.

"He's awake, sir. You're allowed ten minutes with him, but if he becomes distressed, the doctors will tell you to leave."

Harry nodded and got up. He checked his watch. It was 3:30am, Christmas morning.

Both policemen took the lift to ICU and then walked to room four. They entered the room, just as a nurse was leaving.

"He's still very weak, so go easy on him. I'll be outside."

Harry and DC Stewart walked over to the bed. The man lay still, his eyes shut.

"Michael, can you hear me? I'm Detective Chief Inspector Harry Bowe and this is DS Stewart."

The man opened his eyes and regarded both men.

"You here to arrest me?" he asked.

Harry nodded.

"Yes, I am."

"Well, in that case, you better read me my rights."

Harry did so.

"You understand what I've just read you?"

Michael nodded.

"Yes."

"You will remain here until you're well enough to be taken into custody. There, you will be held until trial."

Michael said nothing.

"Can I ask you something?" said Harry, "Do you feel any remorse for the killings you've done?"

Michael regarded Harry.

"I am the protection against the wickedness and snares of the devil. I am a champion of justice. Why would I feel remorse? I have done as God asked. The police are emasculated. They are too busy being woke and wanting to be liked to police properly. The world needs people like me to restore the balance. The irony is your city was safer with me in it than not."

"You will still have to answer for your crimes," said Harry.

A small smile played on Michael's lips.

"I only answer to God. Do your worst, Inspector."

Michael then took a deep breath and quoted.

"Do not fear what you are about to suffer. Behold, the devil is about to throw some of you into prison, that you may be tested, and for ten days you will have tribulation. Be faithful unto death, and I will give you the crown of life. That is from the Book of Revelations 2:10. Now, if you don't mind, I want to sleep."

* * *

Harry left the room with a promise to DC Stewart that he would send relief for him soon. As he walked out into the crisp Christmas morning, he felt a sense of relief, but also one of melancholy.

Michael, or Mick, truly believed that God had instructed him to kill. On the birthday of God's son Jesus, he couldn't allow himself to think that it was true.

If, as Michael had said, there were others on the same mission as he in the world, what would that mean to mankind?

He had to believe in the institution of the police and law and order. Without it, you had anarchy.

Harry drove home in a pensive frame of mind. All he needed now was some sleep tucked up safely next to Carol.

Epilogue

The festive period came and went quietly and Harry enjoyed the few days off. He had eaten too much, drank too much and slept a lot, but felt better for it.

Back at work, the team and he began to write up all the case notes comprehensively.

The report from the hospital was that Michael was making slow but steady progress. None of his wounds had got infected, which could well have been the case, and he was sat up in bed talking coherently.

There was still police presence around the clock on his door and any visitors were strictly vetted and searched before going in to see him.

There hadn't been any visitors so far outside the police and the legal team.

When well enough to be moved, Michael would undergo a string of stringent psychological tests to determine whether he could be diagnosed as sane. Only then, would he be able to stand trial.

When he was well enough, he would be transferred to Clearwater Secure Hospital, a high security psychiatric hospital in the Cotswolds, and would remain there during his examinations.

The case against Michael was pretty damning. The outcome on sentencing depended on whether he was in his right mind when carrying out these brutal killings or whether PTSD had made him psychotic or schizophrenic.

Harry had to play the waiting game. He wasn't the most patient of people when it came to this, but he had no choice.

* * *

Father Matthew returned to St Mathias no worse for wear from his experience and resumed his duties with brief advice from the police about checking out anybody else that he decided to give shelter to.

Father Matthew asked if it would be okay to visit Michael and he was granted permission.

* * *

Duane Rawlings and his buddies were looking at charges of GBH and robbery with violence. Things didn't look good for them, especially in the present climate where a knife was used during the crime. The word was that the judge would make an example of them and throw the book at them.

The death of his father had hit Duane hard. He had revered Charlie and couldn't envisage life without him.

* * *

A week after Christmas, the police raided the Vault Gym and seized thousands of pounds of illegal drugs and four unregistered firearms. At present, the gym is shut down with no plans to reopen anytime soon.

The owner, Edward Lyons, was cleared of any involvement, but has decided to take early retirement and is heading for warmer climates.

* * *

Tommy Good is in custody awaiting trial. The charges are accomplice to murder and perverting the course of justice.

His dreams of being a high-flying editor are in tatters.

Ironically, he did make the big-time tabloids in a way. He was on the front pages for a week or more after word of his arrest.

The Bristol Eye is still running. The editor is now Gloria King, who has worked there for ten years.

* * *

Charlie Rawlings' reign of terror is truly over.

The Albanians never came.

Bristol was a better place for it.

* * *

PC Rob Bailey watched the delectable figure of nurse Molly Ryan getting closer. She was a stunner.

Over the weeks he had been stationed outside Michael's room, he had got to know the nurse pretty well. So well that they had gone out on a date last weekend. A nice meal and a few drinks, then back to Rob's flat for 'coffee'.

He had to admit that he was smitten with Molly.

She was beautiful, clever, funny and had the most incredible ass. She seemed to really like Rob as well.

***

Molly stopped outside room four and gave Rob a seductive smile.

"Hello, handsome. I have a break in five minutes. Do you fancy joining me somewhere quiet?"

Rob felt his pulse quicken. There was nothing in the world that he would have liked more, but he couldn't leave his post. It would cost him his job. Yet...

He looked up into the glorious blue eyes that he could have drowned in.

"Molly, you know I can't do that. It's more than my job's worth."

"Oh, what a shame," said Molly, undoing the top button of her uniform.

Rob didn't fail to see this gesture.

He glanced down the corridor and saw Father Matthew walking towards him.

The priest had visited Michael on several occasions now and read the Bible to him, which the man seemed to enjoy.

"Hello, Father. Back again?" asked Rob.

"Hello, Rob. Yes. Now Michael and I have made peace, I feel dutybound to help a lost soul. I came to read for him again," answered Father Matthew.

PC Rob Bailey suddenly had a thought, which was exactly spiritual.

"Father, would you be okay with Michael for ten minutes on your own? I have a quick errand to run."

The priest smiled.

"Yes, of course. I'll be fine."

Rob got to his feet.

"Great. Any problems, just hit the panic button in there and I'll be back in a flash."

Father Matthew nodded and entered the room.

As soon as he went in, Rob looked at Molly.

"Right. Let's go," he exclaimed.

They both hurried off down the corridor.

* * *

When Father Matthew entered the room, Michael took his headphones off and smiled.

"Father, nice to see you again. Did you bring what I asked?"

"Indeed, I did. A stroke of luck. God has given us a ten-minute window with no police presence outside."

Michael pulled back the covers and gingerly got out of bed. His wounds were healing better than he had let on to the medical staff.

"I'll be glad to shed a few of these layers. I'm rather warm in them," said the priest.

As requested, Father Matthew had worn a double set of clothes.

Michael was now putting on a black cassock over his own trousers and boots. He then borrowed Father Matthew's biretta hat. A large string of rosary beads completed the disguise.

"Ready?" said Father Matthew.

"Ready," replied Michael.

Both men walked out of the room, down the corridor and were out of the hospital unchallenged within minutes.

* * *

Some fifteen minutes later, PC Bailey returned to his post. He glanced through the window and saw the curtains pulled. The shape of Michael was turned away from him covered to the neck with blankets. There was no sign of the priest. Maybe Michael was too tired for a long visit?

It was an hour later when a nurse turned up with meds to be given to the patient that she discovered, to PC Bailey's horror, that Michael was not under the blankets; it was two pillows instead.

He was gone.

* * *

The phone call PC Bailey made to DCI Bowe was not a good one. Bailey had lied about where he was, telling his superior that he had caught a stomach bug in hospital and had to leave his post quickly to use a toilet. He had no choice or risk an accident.

Harry Bowe had read him the riot act, promising that he would address the breach of protocol. For now, he seemed to believe his constable.

Bailey was somewhat relieved, but knew that if hospital CCTV was examined, his lie would be discovered. He was told to come back to headquarters until further notice.

Bailey had told Harry of Father Matthew's visit and the DCI wondered whether he had anything to do with Michael's disappearance.

Hospital CCTV picked up Father Matthew leaving through the front door along with another priest who was walking with a limp.

Michael.

* * *

Father Matthew drove his blue Mini back over to Clifton to a street away from Ruby Webber's place. Michael's van was still parked where he had left it.

Michael regarded the priest.

"Thank you, Father. I owe you so much. You have been a true friend. How can I ever repay you?"

The old priest smiled.

"If your story is true, then have a word with the big man upstairs and ask him to reserve me a place in his company."

Michael extended his hand and Father Matthew shook it.

"Where to now, Michael?" he asked.

"Probably better you don't know, Father, for when the police come asking questions."

With that, Michael got out of the car and then turned around.

"Bye, Father. And God bless you."

Father Matthew watched Michael disappear around the corner to his van. He knew that the police would be paying him a visit, but it was all fundamental now.

While he had been in hospital, a routine examination of his blood had thrown up an anomaly. Further tests had found that he had pancreatic cancer and only had months to live.

The priest had agreed to help Michael because he had nothing to lose. Plus, from some deep conversations with the man, he truly now believed that Michael had killed on the word of God. His faith had been well and truly tested over the last month, but soon he would find out for himself if there was a God.

* * *

The black transit now drove fast through the centre of Bristol. It was 6:00pm on a cold January evening and it was already pitch black. The temperature had dropped drastically throughout the day and the roads had already a sheen of frost on them.

Michael was heading out of Bristol. His plan was to lie low for a while and then, with some money he had tucked away, get a new passport and head back out to Spain to his aunt, before moving further afield again.

The iconic site of the Clifton Suspension Bridge came into view.

He immediately thought of Angela Eccles and his heart felt heavy. Michael would take his guilt to the grave with him. He knew this.

He was heading to join the bridge, but there was a toll charge and they only took card.

Michael was avoiding the motorway and was going to go to North Somerset to the seaside town of Clevedon. There, he had an old army buddy, Sergeant Cliff Warren, ex-SAS, who would be able to help him out with a passport and anything else he needed. No questions asked. He had already provided him the transit van previously. He was a useful man to know.

Michael put his foot down hard on the accelerator as he approached the toll barrier. Without slowing, he smashed right through. As he did so, he momentarily lost control of the van as it hit a patch of ice.

He hit the brakes hard, but the van skidded badly and careened towards the edge of the bridge. Michael swerved to avoid a cyclist and then a woman with a pushchair. The van hit the side barrier hard. It turned onto its side and came to a halt.

Michael was stunned. Not having fully healed from his wounds, the new impact did not sit favourably with his already battered body. It took him minutes to realise where he was. He touched his head and felt blood.

He unclipped his seatbelt, opened the door and climbed out, falling onto the ground. Traffic on the bridge had ground to a halt and Michael could hear the approaching sirens.

He looked around him.

He had nowhere to run, so he climbed up and out onto the side of the bridge itself. He looked down into the murky waters of the river Avon, which flowed on out into the Bristol Channel. He could also see the surrounding craggy cliffs of Avon Gorge and the busy Portway beneath him.

***

Harry picked up his mobile and answered the call from DS Diane Rose.

"Sir, we have news of a road traffic accident on the Clifton Suspension Bridge. A van has hit the barriers and overturned."

Harry was impatient, wanting news on the escaped Michael, not an RTA.

"Yes, and…"

"It's a black transit van and the plates are false. I think it's Michael," answered Rose.

Now, Harry's interest was aroused.

"Go on," he urged.

"A man has got out of the car and climbed over the side of the bridge. Description fits our man."

"Right, get out there quickly. I'm on my way," answered Harry.

The game was on again.

* * *

Michael looked down at the water, then back at the gathered crowd and also the police.

A black cop, who introduced himself as DS Kevin Rowland, had tried to persuade him to come back in.

Michael couldn't do that. It was over. It was time to go back and meet God.

His job was complete.

He knew that he should have died on that operating table and he had only been living on borrowed time.

There was nowhere left for a man like Michael to go.

He certainly wasn't going to rot in prison or a loony bin.

* * *

Suddenly, a man pushed through the crowd. He recognised his face as the police chief who had arrested him at the hospital. His name slipped his mind, but somewhere in his head, he thought of a sweet.

The man stepped forward.

"Michael, it's over. Come down. There's nowhere left to run. Do the right thing and give it up. The tactical firearms unit are on the way. They'll take you down if you resist arrest."

Michael looked around again.

How had it all come to this? One minute, he was fighting in a war in Afghanistan. Now, he was hanging off Clifton Suspension Bridge in Bristol.

He remembered coming up here as a kid with his parents on a day out, which would also encompass a visit to the zoological gardens followed by dinner in McDonald's.

The bridge truly was a work of art by Isambard Kingdom Brunel. 1,352 feet long and 75 metres above the water.

He had heard of many people jumping off of the bridge. None, as far as he knew, had survived.

Suddenly, a van pulled up and armed police poured out, guns at the ready.

Harry looked towards Michael.

"Come on, son. Give it up."

Michael smiled at Harry, then stood upright and saluted him, before jumping out into the night sky.

Harry stood still transfixed on the space where Michael had been stood a minute ago.

He shook his head in dismay.

The body would be hard to retrieve, what with the muddy banks and strong current.

There was never going to be a good ending to this case, but he couldn't help feeling empathy for the man.

The army had used Michael and Tommy Good had then done the same.

Michael had been a vulnerable man, but also an extremely dangerous one. He wondered if men like him truly could belong back in normal society. How many more Michaels were walking the streets ready to explode?

Harry pulled up his coat collar against the cold wind and made his way back to his car.

It was over.

Michael had dished out his own justice and, on this occasion, chosen to take his own life.

* * *

The cold water enveloped Michael's body. It took his breath away and it felt like a giant vice was tightening around his chest.

He sank deep to the bottom and his lungs took in huge quantities of murky water.

Suddenly, he felt the calming sensation wash over him once again and he saw the corridor with the light at the end.

Michael began to walk slowly down it. It felt like he was effortlessly floating.

He then heard a familiar voice. The voice of God. Was he welcoming him to heaven? Was he pleased with his work? Was this his final moments on earth?

Michael embraced it.

He then heard the voice say.

"Michael, wait…"

* * *

Six weeks later found Harry and Carol getting some winter sunshine in Marbella, Spain. They were staying at an all-inclusive hotel overlooking the beach and the gorgeous blue sea.

Harry was sat on a terraced bar sipping an ice-cold beer as Carol swam in the rooftop pool.

This was just what the doctor ordered. The warm sun on his face felt good.

The case of 'The Avenging Angel' was now old news. Things had moved on. New cases to solve.

The body of Michael was never found, although it was not unusual as many people jumping from the bridge were washed out into the Bristol Channel and lost forever.

The case had caught the public imagination and in two weeks' time, Harry was going to be on television as a documentary called *The Avenging Angel* was going to be made.

Harry would have a starring role in it. Something he wasn't particular comfortable with.

He tried to push the thought to the back of his mind for now.

***

Harry looked out to sea and saw people swimming or playing ball. Some small boats were dotted on the horizon. Idyllic.

They had been here a week and they had another one to go.

Thoughts of early March weather in the UK with its winds and rain were far away and life for now was good.

His attention was then drawn to a lone surfer.

A well-built guy. Long hair. Looked a typical surfing type.

Harry watched him ride the waves with ease into the shore, then get off his board and begin to walk up the sand.

Something about his gait and posture struck a chord with the policeman.

The surfer disappeared from view and that was when Harry realised that the man had a pronounced limp on his left leg.

Coincidence. Surely?

Other Books by the Author

If you enjoyed this book, then check out other
stories by Kevin. Read a little about them
on the following pages.
Available online at Amazon, Waterstones
and all good bookstores.

For more information, visit www.kevinohagan.com
or join the group, Kevin O'Hagan
Author's Corner on Facebook.

Battlescars

Tony Slade Novel number 1

Some wounds run deep. Can they ever heal?

Tony Slade sits in a coffee shop waiting. He is reflecting on his dark and violent past. He is waiting for the woman he loves, but he is also waiting for the man who wants him dead. Who will reach him first? The clock is ticking...

Tony Slade is used to dealing with violence and death. He has made a career out of it. From boxer to bouncer, paratrooper, and mercenary to minder. But now, he is getting older and he wants out. He has miraculously found love and he has one last chance at happiness, but it will come with a price. The woman he loves is not his; she belongs to a very dangerous man. A man who you don't want to cross. But Tony is ready to risk it all on one last roll of the dice before a powder keg of violence explodes.

But that is not all. Unknown to him, there is another threat coming his way. One that he will not see until the last moment. Who will get out alive?

Tough times call for tough people. Tony Slade is one such person.

No Hiding Place

Tony Slade Novel number 2

You can run but you can't hide forever.

They say time is a great healer. But for Tony Slade time is running out. The physical scars are healing, but the mental ones are still raw. Waking up in hospital after the coffee shop massacre and finding he has cheated death; he needs to know why. But he has now become a man everybody wants to question. All he wants to do is disappear forever, but some people will not let that happen.

Suddenly, Tony is hounded by the press and media. He is also trailed by the tenacious DCI Wyatt and hunted by a psychotic killer who is relentless, and hell bent on revenge.

Tony Slade is in hiding recovering from the bullet wounds and the trauma of recent events that have changed his life forever. Hiding on the tiny, isolated island of *Graig O Mor* in the Bristol Channel, Tony knows that it is only a matter of time until he is found. Then, he will have to stop running and make a stand against an enemy who will not give up. It will become a matter of life and death.

A storm is coming from the mainland
to the Island of Graig O Mor.

Last Stand

Tony Slade Novel number 3

Blood is thicker than water

Tony Slade is living in the Canary Islands. He is resting and soaking up the sun. He is keeping his head down under an assumed identity and trying to forget the last few traumatic years where he has experienced love, violence, heartbreak and death.

Tony is a survivor. An ex-paratrooper and mercenary who has seen more than his fair share of action, but those days are well behind him now. Or so he thought.

He is no longer a young man and the fire that used to burn like an inferno in his belly is now just flickering. Tony is looking for a quiet life into retirement when he receives a shocking and lifechanging piece of news. A secret that has been buried for years has suddenly came to light.

This secret will force Tony out of hiding to return to the UK and back into the violent world of gangsters, drugs and crime.

Pursued all the time by an old nemesis, Tony must pull all his fighting skills together to face a dangerous and deadly drug lord who has something of his that he wants back at any cost. Tony knows that blood will spill in one final stand.

This time, it's personal

Killing Time

Joe Regan novel 1

Ex-Scotland Yard policeman DCI Joe Regan had retired from the force after a particularly vicious attempt on his life, which had him on the critical list in hospital, but his gritty Gaelic spirit and resolve helped him recover.

Now leading a new life running an antiques emporium in the sleepy town of Oakcombe in the West Country, he is trying to put his past behind him. But unknown to Joe, a burglary at the nearby country home of famous TV celebrity Ron Goodwin opens up a nasty can of worms in the form of something hidden within an antique clock which finds its way to his shop.

This something could ruin Ron Goodwin's career just as he is about to crack America. The dark secrets contained within the clock cannot afford to fall into the wrong hands, so it must be found at all costs, even if it means murder.

Joe Regan suddenly finds himself embroiled in a race to find the clock and its contents as they go missing, before a hired killer who will stop at nothing does. But when Joe inadvertently stumbles across the secret, he now becomes the next target.

The clock is ticking, and time is running out.

A Change of Heart

*Can a heart transplant victim inherit
the characteristics of their donor?*

Simon Winter is a prime candidate for a heart attack. Middle aged, sedentary and grossly overweight. His lifestyle is driving him to an early grave, but he is ignoring all the signs until it is too late.

He has a failed marriage behind him, a boring job and a fear of violence and blood. He has lived a safe and uneventful life, avoiding confrontation and danger until now where this is all about to change dramatically.

Eddie Prince is an ex-professional boxer and minor television celebrity. He has had a turbulent life out of the ring, which has resulted in prison time. Money has come and gone as he has a gambling addiction, which results in him owing a lot of money to some bad people. He has run away to what he hopes is a better life, but his old life is about to catch up with him, resulting in dire circumstances.

These two men are about to connect in a way they could never have dreamed of. Two men at different ends of the spectrum. Two men who are chalk and cheese. Two men who have nothing in common until one inherits the other's heart after a transplant.

Now one will use the other as a vessel of revenge to find the man who murdered him and settle a score with shocking conclusions.

Blood Tracks

At one time in the 1980s, Stormtrooper were the most successful rock band on the planet. Everything they touched turned to gold. But among all the fame was jealousy and greed. This resulted in the sacking of their iconic lead singer Jimmy Parrish for drug usage, which endangered the band's continued success.

Sometime later after a bitter break-up, Jimmy Parrish apparently committed suicide in mysterious circumstances. His body was never found. A proposed warts and all book on the band that he had been approached to write would now never happen, a blessing for some.

The Mark 2 line-up of the band went on to have global success and entered the Rock and Roll Hall of Fame as one of the biggest rock bands of all time. Even when they finally split up, the spectre of Jimmy Parrish never fully went away.

Fast forward twenty years, the band have reformed to record a new album. They are heading for the remote island of Ruma off the Outer Hebrides. Ruma is a wild isolated place of mystery and intrigue. They will stay at the grand house of a reclusive film director who has a state-of-the-art recording studio in the bowels of the building.

Storm Alec is due to hit the island. It will cut it and its inhabitants off from the rest of civilisation.

But worse is to come as a mysterious killer lurks within the walls of the house hellbent on murdering each and every member of the band and their recording crew.

Who is it and what is their motive?

There is nowhere to run and nowhere to hide. Nobody is coming to help.

As the body count rises, who - if anybody - can survive.

Making a hit record can sometimes be murder.

The Key to Murder

Is money the root of all evil?

Imagine that you found a key. A key that opened a locker. A locker that contained a holdall. A holdall that contained money. A lot of money. £350,000 to be exact in used untraceable notes.

What would you do?

Put it back in the locker and walk away? Contact the police? Or take it?

It is a life changing sum.

But what if that money belonged to a dangerous man? A man who will stop at nothing to get it back. He will relentlessly track you down and anybody who gets in his way will suffer.

This is what happens when the worlds of three men clash.

Ronnie Moon, Tommy Scott and Adam Lucas are all involved in a deadly game of Cat and Mouse. Each want the money for different reasons.

The hunt is on, but who will survive?

Their greed and ambition could just be the Key to Murder.

If you want to know what man is really like, take notice of what he is really like when he loses money.

Murder in Store

"You know what they say about curiosity, don't you?"

Chris Cooper is nicknamed the 'Nighthawk'. He and his friends are urban explorers. They love to enter abandoned buildings and structures and search them, especially at night when nobody else is around. The activity is illegal, but it gives them such a buzz that it becomes addictive. They love to flirt with danger.

Eddie Creed is on the run to Bristol. He has inadvertently crossed 'Big Baz' Watkins, a London criminal with a nasty reputation. Eddie only wanted to help the girl, but now his world is turned upside down as three hitmen are on his trail. Their agenda is to kill him.

On this particular cold winter's evening, Chris and his friends will enter and explore the empty store of the iconic Radley's in Bristol city centre.

On this same night. Eddie Creed, who is being chased down by the hitmen, seeks refuge and finds it in the same store. When the killers also enter the store and block off its only exit, a shocking and horrifying series of events begins to unfold.

Suddenly, the worlds of Eddie Creed and Chris Cooper and his friends collide as mayhem and murder occurs. Now, they are all running for their lives as they are relentlessly hunted down.

There will be murder in store!

Buried Secrets
Joe Regan Novel 2

What if an enduring legend proved to be true? A legend that most people dismissed in the same way as Sasquatch, the Loch Ness Monster, Excalibur and the Tooth Fairy?

What if this legend spoke of priceless religious artefacts buried and hidden by Celtic monks from the invading barbarian hordes sailing to the British Isles? Treasures so cleverly hidden that they have lay undiscovered for centuries, waiting to be found.

Professor Declan Byrne of Trinity College Dublin thinks that he has evidence to the whereabouts of such treasures. Evidence that he has outlined in a journal.

If true, it will be the find of the century.

But somebody else has found this out and wants the journal at any costs. They will stop at nothing to get their hands on it. Even murder. And so, the hunt to find the treasure begins. Desperate measures will be taken to be the first person to find it.

Joe Regan, former DCI in the Metropolitan Police and now antiques dealer, is holidaying on the south coast of Ireland with his girlfriend Maggie. He is retracing his family's heritage and reliving a few memories from his childhood there.

He had not planned on being suddenly caught up in a web of mystery and crime concerning Celtic treasures, drug smuggling and murder. But it seems trouble follows Joe wherever he goes, and he is going to have to all his resources and experience to keep himself one step ahead of the hunt and, more importantly, stay alive.

About the Author

Kevin O'Hagan lives just outside Bristol with his wife. He has three grown-up children and five grandchildren.

Kevin has had a passion for writing since he was a child, but has no formal writing training. Everything he has learnt has been a personal voyage of discovery.

One of his favourite sayings is, "If you want to get better at writing, then write."

Avenging Angel is his tenth work of fiction to date.

Kevin is a semi-retired world-renowned martial artist. He holds an 8th Dan black belt in Ju Jutsu after more than 49 years of training and teaching. These days, he still teaches part-time.

His hobbies are reading, writing, playing guitar, going to the gym and travelling.

www.kevinohagan.com for more information.